MURDER IN WOLFCLEUGH WOODS

An addictive crime mystery full of twists

ROY LEWIS

Arnold Landon Mysteries Book 16

Originally published as *Dead Secret*

Revised edition 2022
Joffe Books, London
www.joffebooks.com

First published in Great Britain in 2001
as *Dead Secret*

This paperback edition was first published
in Great Britain in 2022

ISBN: 978-1-80405-277-8

PROLOGUE

There were bodies in the woods.

It had always been a dark place, a revered and feared place, an area of mystery and shadows. It had not always been shrouded in undergrowth, crowned with ancient oaks, magnificent spreading ash and the gnarled remnants of old, decaying birch and elm. The huge powers at the earth's core had lifted up the hill over the aeons, and a dune of periglacial wind-blown sand had formed in the large hollow left by the retreating ice. Rains and storms had worked their own magic on the swampy plateau: an acid soil had formed, accumulations of peat had built up in the wetter areas of pools and damper hummocks, and among the fungal rust grew anemone and ranunculus, lychnis, lotus and potentilla, and marsh grasses spread thickly along the nutrient-enriched marginal edges of the bog.

Gradually, as the centuries passed, the mire retreated and the drier adjacent land rose slightly as vegetation thickened, pine and alder, birch and ash intruded, and secondary woodland clothed the slope. Meadowsweet and docks, bracken and ivy spread through the area and the oaks grew tall among the hazel and the willows. It was still a mixed woodland centuries later, open in character, light enough for the flowering ilex and corylus to flourish.

Then Man came to the hill.

For a thousand years he worked at the edges of the bog, clearing part of the hill, disturbing the light soils. From time to time, climatic deterioration caused the hill to be abandoned for agricultural purposes and the natural forces led to change in the bog characteristics and the vegetation. The water beetles retreated into the thick, mossy swamp; *Scirtidae* larvae overwintered in litter, under bark and among the rush stems, and the moist, boggy ground retained the heads and thoraxes of ground beetles, preserved in the damp peat, and the Neolithic men on the hill came to recognise the magical properties of the swamp. A man could die there, be drowned in the swamp on a dark, stormy night and many years later would be cast out, his skin leathery, but his body otherwise miraculously preserved. It was a magic place.

The bog was seen as a living thing. It refused to retain its boundaries and sometimes an enormous mass of fluid substance would move, spreading itself to take possession of the plain. The people who lived at its boundaries saw it as a moving hill, terrified inhabitants watching in awe as the bog grew, swallowed up the wooden and turf and stone dwellings; the translocation of the bog under heavy rains caused by a raised mire and collapse of a water-saturated dome.

But to the men of the hill it was the gods, and the gods required sacrifice.

Over the centuries slaves, captives taken in battle, would be taken there. Stags, pigs, wild, savage-tusked boars would be sacrificed in a plea to the gods of the skies and of the earth, the wind and the stars — and of the woods. The ritual was all. Shamans would intone their whirling incantations, the heady smoke would rise, and under the full moon the shadows of the oaks and encircling woodland were deep und mysterious and sinister.

But there was always death: the garrotting rope, the swift slash of the knife blade and then the immersion in the swamp. Sometimes the body would be left in the open, but the unconsolidated sphagnum mat would soon cover it, hiding it from view, a return of the flesh to the earth.

As the centuries passed, when the ice had all melted away, wolves dominated the hills, moving among the forest of hazel and birch on the upper fells, hunting down in the valleys and under the thick cover of oak and elm. And on the hill the Moss shrank, the secondary woodland advanced, and Man's view of his place in the order of things changed. The old religions had gone and other gods held sway.

But some things did not change. The woodland that crowned the hill was still a place of fear and superstition. It came to be called Wolfcleugh Hill, an eerie, wind-whistled place resounding with whispered stories of terror, echoing against the distant backdrop of high, bold rocks to the east. It seemed to epitomise the area with its hanging woods, deep pools and high crags, and yet it was different. It was heavy with deep, ancient instincts, origins now lost, reasons scattered with the incantations of long-dead shamans.

The mire remained, ice-rimmed, fog-shrouded in winter, smaller now and shadowed by the menacing shoulder of the woodland.

But the bodies were there. Local knowledge had it but who began the stories, who passed them on, no one now knew. The mists of centuries obscured the reality and the ritual was gone.

Wolfcleugh Woods remained.

CHAPTER ONE

1

They filed into the university hall, an oddly assorted group both in age and appearance. They took their seats on the dais and shuffled uncertainly under the television lights, peering with a certain anxiety towards the people seated in front of them.

The first two rows facing them had been taken by local reporters, a few radio hacks, some writers from historical and archaeological magazines, and local politicians from County Hall who saw this as an opportunity to obtain some credit for a discovery in which they had played no part whatsoever. Television coverage, announced in advance, had also played its part in gathering an audience: even if they were not particularly interested in the topic, there were still people to whom the thought of actually appearing on television was thrilling and worth coming along for, to listen to a description of something they had little interest in. They shuffled in anticipation now, eyes fixed on the group on the dais.

The woman seated at the centre of the group lifted a small gavel and tapped it on the table. 'I should begin by introducing myself,' she announced. 'I am Dr Diane Power.' She hesitated, as though expecting applause for the achievement. When it did not come, she went on, 'I am leading the

6

team that is presenting the first report on the bog body . . .
described by the popular press as the Wolf Man . . .'

Seated towards the back of the room, Arnold Landon
smiled. Ever since the ancient body had been discovered
in the mire below Wolfcleugh Hill there had competition
among the tabloids to come up with an appropriate name.
It was one of the local reporters who had finally coined the
sobriquet of Wolf Man: the body's hirsute appearance and
animal pelt cloak had inspired the thought. The name had
now been taken up by all and sundry, though Arnold himself
did not think it a particularly appropriate one.

He sat and watched Dr Diane Power as she began to
introduce the other members of the group. He had never
met her, but knew of her academic and archaeological reputation. She was a tall woman, heavy-shouldered, somewhat
mannish in appearance, dressed in a no-nonsense tweed skirt
and sweater. Her shoes were broad and sensible. Her hair
was dark, cut short, and piercing blue eyes glinted with a
certain hostility above a firm nose, as though she expected
trouble and was ready for it. She had a reputation for being
short-tempered, but she was well respected and had a sound
background in archaeological research.

'Dr Buckley, on my left, has been conducting a review
of the peat stratigraphy and age of the body . . .' she was
explaining. The thin-faced man on her left nodded, flickering
a hooded glance around the room. 'Dr Wells, next to him,
is reporting on the soft tissue remains and the bone erosion
findings . . .'

There seemed to be little soft tissue on Dr Wells himself:
a desiccated man in his late fifties, he leaned back in his chair
with a bored air, idly flicking a pencil between his fingers as
though demonstrating his lack of interest in the whole pro-
ceedings. But, thought Arnold, exposure of this kind to the
press was necessary if funding was to be sought.

'Then we have Dr Scandle, who is responsible for exam-
ination of the pollen samples obtained from faecal, colonic,
gastro-intestinal, duodenal and rectal residue—'

'Sounds like a load of crap to me,' one of the reporters exclaimed loudly in the front row and there was a subdued ripple of nervous giggling which quickly subsided under the glare of Diane Power's formidable eye.

'Dr Pinter deals with the chemical and microbiological aspects of the preservation process, and Dr Elliott the analysis of adipocere samples . . .'

Arnold's attention wandered. The discovery of the bog body, almost two years ago now, had been a sensation at the time but had not involved the department in which he was employed, Museums and Antiquities. The work had been the result of a university investigation team, funded by a bequest from an eccentric Irish lady from Hartlepool called Maggie Cleugh who was convinced that her ancestors had once owned the bog and woods, and that the history of her family could be found in the depths of the mire. No one at the university disputed the issue or argued with her: they took her money and mounted the investigation.

Now, things were changing somewhat and Karen Stannard, the Acting Director of the department of Museums and Antiquities, had asked Arnold to attend the press briefing. Maggie Cleugh was dead, the money from her bequest was drying up and there was political mileage to be gained by the county taking some part in the whole process.

'The original discovery of the Wolf Man was made, of course, by a Mr Middleton, who was digging for peat under a licence unwisely granted by the council,' Diane Power was saying. 'Unwise, because such activity can be described only as vandalism, destroying a precious cultural heritage, rendering impossible the revealing, layer by layer, of our past. However, that work has now stopped, because of the discovery of the body . . .'

After a lot of debate and compensation paid to an irate businessman who saw his profits from the garden industry disappearing, Arnold thought.

'The first thing seen by Mr Middleton was a foot, unfortunately cut off by the mechanical digger. This would have been about eighteen inches below the surface of the peat. Subsequent investigation of the site led to the discovery of what appeared to be a human body, so the police were called in . . .'

There had always been peat-digging at Wolfcleugh, Arnold knew, and many finds of the remains of cows and sheep who, ranging for food, had been unfortunate enough to slip into the pits and trenches of the bog, to starve, suffocate and eventually be preserved there. Some years ago there had been found a primitive, ancient roadway made of logs and timbers placed end to end, with sleepers across, and there had long been tales of the buck stealers, poachers and fishers who used the natural and ready products of the country, as one antiquary had put it, to make traps and snares, besoms and straw beehives: a race apart and many lost in the fog-shrouded bogs, it was said.

'So we have the remains,' Diane Power continued, 'of an adult male, some thirty years of age. We cannot be certain of how he was deposited in the bog but he was found—'

'Minus a foot,' interrupted the self-appointed humourist in the front.

'—lying on his right side, legs drawn up and arms bent. The leather cap and belt he wore are well preserved, the wolf-skin cape has been well recorded, part of the upper body had collapsed as a result of bone and flesh deterioration, and the skin was folded. However, the head was in good condition, bearded, long-haired, and the sexual organs and the stomach were also well preserved. This has given us a great deal to work upon.'

'A man of parts,' the humourist muttered *sotto voce*, and someone in the second row tut-tutted.

Arnold glanced around as Dr Power went on to discuss the remains of the Wolf Man's last meal — porridge of barley, linseed and willowherb seeds. The audience was silent now, fascinated by the account of what life must have been like millennia ago, with a diet of wild seeds such as fat hen, corn spurrey, hemp nettle and mustard. But there were

9

stirrings in the front row: the reporters wanted more sensational information.

'But what do you have to tell us about the manner of his death?' one finally interrupted.

Dr Diane Power was not pleased. She fixed the man with a withering glance, which suggested that she had more important matters to concentrate on than sensational trivia. But she needed the funding. 'We have concluded that he had been struck on the left temple and his right shin had been fractured. A noose of braided leather was found around his throat. It left a furrow on the skin at the sides and at the throat. Not at the nape. From this we can deduce he was not strangled, as some reports have suggested. This was not a ritual murder, we believe, it was a hanging.'

'But the throat was cut, I understand,' the reporter persisted.

Diane Power, slightly exasperated, realised from the shuffling in the front rows that her scholarly exposition was not going to satisfy the media. With an air of resignation she gave them what they wanted. 'Interpretation of bog body discoveries generally underlines several common features: pre-immersion strangulation, garrotting, beheading. These comprise the standard components of Iron Age watery ritual theories.'

'Did they fall or were they pushed, I suppose,' the reporter interrupted.

'That's the lay discussion,' Diane Power said drily. 'But the current fashion that ascribes all bog finds to votive or ritual deposition ignores discoveries of prehistoric artefacts in the same areas. To argue necessarily ritual deposition of the bodies, when common objects are also found, is surely mistaken — the sites were not always seen as . . . *special*.'

'But—'

'This man was hanged. He might have been a common criminal. It might have been practice to cast such criminals into a quagmire. On the other hand maybe peat was heaped over the body to prevent the escape of unpleasant odours from decomposition. We cannot know.'

'But ritual deposition is now well documented—' Diane Power snorted. 'There is also an assumption that the people who buried bodies in bogs actually anticipated body preservation. But have you ever thought how difficult it might have been to ensure such preservation? There are climatic problems in maintaining a constantly high water table for anaerobia, essential for preservation. The fact is, sir, that flesh putrefies when constant immersion is not maintained. Carrion-eating organisms in aerobic surface parts attack the body and consume important parts within a short time. The body thus must sink quickly or be buried well below the effects of seasonal changes in the water table, if it is to be preserved.'

'And the Wolf Man?'

Diane Power leaned back in her chair, shaking her head 'He was just . . . hanged. Probably thrown thereafter into the mud at the bottom of a pond or bog hole. That's all we can say.'

'And now, what about the future, Dr Power?'

'How do you mean?'

The reporter stood up. Arnold knew him: he worked for the Northern Echo and wrote occasional pieces on the work of the department of Museums and Antiquities.

'Well, I understand that the bequest from Mrs Maggie Cleugh, which has funded your work over the last two years, has now dried up. Does this mean that you unfortunately will not be able to continue with your investigations?'

'The university has other funding sources. I am confident we can continue with our analysis of the body of your Wolf Man.'

'I'm sure the university will be able to do that. But,' the reporter persisted, 'that's not really what I'm driving at. I believe I'm right in saying that there is a 1535 reference to a bog burst at Wolfcleugh Moss and discovery of some bodies, that were later reburied. Then again, in 1771 we have a similar account, where it is recorded that a woman in a state of so-called perfect preservation was discovered. If we accept a history of ritual deposition over five thousand years—'

'Your timescale is about right, if not your ritual deposition assumption,' Diane Power remarked drily.

'—is it not highly likely that there are many more discoveries to be made in Wolfcleugh Moss?'

There was a short, expectant silence. Diane Power glanced around at her panel, her lips thinning. 'Both I and my colleagues all feel there is a high probability that there are other finds to be made.'

'So I come back to my question,' the reporter insisted. 'What of the future?'

'That,' Diane Power responded grimly, 'is beyond my brief today.'

'But it is an important question.'

* * *

They all silently acknowledged it, as they sat in the conference room the next day. The late afternoon sun slanted through the window, flecks of gold in the air, dust specks drifting in a light, inconsequential dance that led nowhere, rising and falling like the argument. Karen Stannard, elegant and beautifully dressed, was seated to Arnold's right, her skin tanned, her slim legs crossed, her eyes watchful and non-committal. She glanced at Portia Tyrrel, well settled in now as her assistant.

It had been a matter of surprise to the gossips in the department that Karen Stannard, tall, confident, almost arrogantly beautiful, should have chosen to enlist to her team a woman as striking as Portia. Short black hair, pale olive-skinned, small-breasted and slimly built, she could turn heads in a room as well as Karen Stannard, but perhaps the older woman saw her almost as a foil: two beautiful women, but different in their beauty, and in their status. Nevertheless, Arnold suspected that Karen Stannard now had reservations about the wisdom of having appointed Portia. The Eurasian assistant from Singapore clearly had a mind and an opinion of her own, and was not averse to expressing her thoughts openly. Arnold had detected a rising tension between the two women during the last few months. It might have been due to Karen Stannard's own ambitions, for she clearly still laboured under the gnawing anxiety that she might yet not be confirmed in the appointment as director of the department. Portia was not a rival at that level, of course, but every time she disagreed with her director it was a pinprick to Karen Stannard's self-confidence. And she disagreed with her now.

Arnold had never previously felt that Karen lacked self-confidence, but Portia Tyrrel seemed to have the ability to get under her skin, irritate her in an odd way.

'I'm not at all certain we should get the department involved,' Karen Stannard doubted.

'But we *are* involved,' Portia insisted, her almond eyes narrowed. 'We've been asked by the chief executive to make a report.'

'Making a report does not necessarily mean taking a position,' Karen Stannard averred.

Portia's displeasure was clear. 'I disagree. There's little point in the exercise, otherwise. And Wolfcleugh is an important issue. If we don't take a firm stand much damage could be done.'

'As I said—'

'You delegated the reporting function to me. But I have no departmental guidance. I'll have to comment upon the report in half an hour and—'

'That's not quite right,' Karen Stannard interrupted frostily. 'I've read your report, Portia. And your conclusions. They are . . . impassioned. I am not certain they are properly phrased in the context they are to be placed. But . . . I will be doing the presentation, not you. A presentation to the chief executive and the others who will be present requires a certain tact . . . an awareness of the nuances . . . It requires rather more . . . balance than you seem to be able to manage.'

There was a short, edgy silence. Portia glanced at Arnold, as though for support. He knew what she was feeling: she had written a sharply argued and properly researched paper, under the directions of the Acting Director, but it would be Karen Stannard herself who would take any kudos that might be going for its presentation. Though, Arnold considered wryly, if it were to be criticised, he had no doubt the buck would swiftly be passed back to Portia Tyrrel. And Portia knew that too.

'So you yourself, Miss Stannard, have taken no position on this debate,' she said icily.

There was a sweetness in Karen Stannard's smile, which was belied by the mockery in her eyes. 'I can't afford to take a position, Portia. I have to take into account the political considerations, rise above the basic arguments, look at the wider scene . . .'

Such as the impact the report might have upon her personal aspirations, Arnold thought. This was a battle he was not entering, because it could not be won.

Half an hour later, as the three of them sat in a grim silence, the others began to arrive in the conference room. Coffee was served: Arnold noted that Powell Frinton, the chief executive, seemed to have acquired a rather more elegant set of coffee cups recently, belying the almost ascetic view he seemed to have of life. Perhaps he was changing as he neared retirement, but Arnold doubted it.

The chairman of the Environmental Planning Committee, Councillor Sammy Jonson, entered with two other men, followed by Powell Frinton himself. Jonson was short and flabby, an ex-dockyard worker from Sunderland whose muscle had turned to fat as he had achieved the good life, living off expenses as a council member and attending exuberant dinners offered by those who sought to subvert planning regulations relating to the environment. He participated in such jollities with enthusiasm. The other two men were strangers to Arnold. He observed them as introductions were made.

Ken Stafford was middle-aged, lean, good-looking in a craggy sort of way, with a receding hairline and sharp eyes. His mouth was of the kind that smiled easily, but not in conjunction with his eyes: they remained the eyes of a businessman, watchful and suspicious, unwilling to believe in luck, conscious only of the need to summarise, weigh up, seek out weakness in another man's defences. He was dressed in an expensive dark suit; his cream shirt was sharp; his tie plain and unadorned. He exuded an air of watchful confidence and his handshake was firm, his voice deep and controlled.

'And this is my associate, Colm Graham,' he said to Arnold.

Graham didn't fit in the gathering, somehow. He had the shoulders of a prize-fighter and a nose to match. His slitted eyes suggested he was waiting to take a boxer's advantage, waiting for the opening. He had a closed face, nothing given away, and his body seemed well-honed, gym-trained. His suit was careful rather than expensive and tight around the chest. They were an ill-assorted pair, Arnold thought, and yet perhaps they had matching strengths. Ken Stafford, the smooth, precise and determined businessmen; Colm Graham, with the suggestion of controlled, committed violence.

'So, shall we be seated?' Powell Frinton suggested in his reedy voice. His eyes rested on Arnold briefly as though he was wondering why three representatives were required from the department of Museums and Antiquities. 'Councillor Jonson, perhaps you would like to take the chair?'

Councillor Jonson would. He moved into it ponderously, his appreciative glances taking in both Karen Stannard and Portia Tyrrel. He ignored Arnold. 'Now the way I understand it, Chief Executive,' he began, 'the submission that Mr Stafford has made to my committee, on behalf of Shangri-La Enterprises, has been looked at by your department, and is now also the subject of a report from Museums and Antiquities—'

'Who have a certain overriding responsibility in this area,' Powell Frinton suggested.

Karen Stannard smiled thinly. Arnold guessed she would not be taking that responsibility too seriously if it meant she could gain something from ignoring it.

'Perhaps Miss Stannard would like to introduce the report?' Councillor Jonson suggested, sliding his glance over

Karen Stannard's tanned throat to the neckline of her blouse, top button undone, first swelling of her breast exposed. Arnold smiled. Karen never missed an obvious opportunity.

'I don't propose to read a report,' Karen Stannard said sweetly, 'but rather to circulate a summary and make a few observations. And please, in making those observations, if Mr Stafford or yourself, Chairman, wish to correct me on any of my statements, please feel free . . .' There was a short appreciative silence, some nods of assent, then she went on: 'The issue would seem to centre around the proposals made by Shangri-La Enterprises for the construction of one of their complexes in the valley to the north of Wolfcleugh Hill.'

Arnold was familiar enough with the Shangri-La Country Park developments. They were not unlike many that had sprung up in France and England: an hotel complex equipped with a properly supervised swimming pool, health centre, gymnasium, stables and other sporting facilities both indoor and outdoor; a limited number of upmarket chalets; local woodland; shooting rights on nearby fells; a place where every whim was catered for, devoted to middle-class visitor aspirations, family holidays where well-heeled parents could park their children safely while they indulged themselves in the hedonistic pursuits of their choice, either on site, or within the licensed areas nearby.

'The construction work is already under way,' Ken Stafford intervened smoothly, 'and is going well. But we must have a decision soon on the access road.'

'The original access, as I understand it,' Karen Stannard continued, 'was to be by way of Brathstone Village, but local protests and the narrowness of the Roman bridge at that location have led the authority to seek some other solution. The new approach that is suggested—'

'And supported by the Planning Committee,' Stafford said quietly.

'The new access route crosses behind Brathstone and loops across the river by Claygate, to approach the valley by way of Wolfcleugh Hill.'

'It *skirts* Wolfcleugh Hill,' Stafford said firmly.

There was a short silence, as Karen Stannard looked at her notes and Jonson looked at her neckline. She would be trying to gauge feelings now, Arnold thought, work out just where Powell Frinton and Jonson might stand in all this. At last, she looked up. 'The issue, of course, has been clouded by the discovery of the bog body, popularly known as the Wolf Man, in nearby Wolfcleugh Moss. There is now a considerable gathering of opinion in the academic world, led by Dr Diane Power, that Wolfcleugh Moss is likely to lead to numerous more important finds and is a site to be cherished. This was the tenor of her presentation the other evening. There is the matter of funding for a more intensive investigation of the site, but I understand Dr Power is approaching both the European funding bodies and our own—'

'It's all pie in the sky,' Stafford interrupted caustically. 'She'll not get the money and in any case her arguments are irrelevant. We are not proposing that the access road be driven across Wolfcleugh Moss: that would be impractical anyway. The roadway would be on the higher ground, skirting the woodland, well away from where she found her bog body. It wouldn't affect the site.'

'It depends what you mean by the site,' Portia Tyrrel burst out, ignoring the sharp glance thrown at her by Karen Stannard and that of Councillor Jonson, who turned his piggy eyes on her with quite a different expression. 'I've discussed the matter at length with Dr Power and the rest of her team. Wolfcleugh Moss is, in modern times, a great deal smaller than it was in the past. The bogland has been retreating: depredations from peat-cutting, drainage and agriculture have caused an extension of the woodland over the centuries, a creeping down the hill, a withdrawal and drying out of the bog. The site should be seen as inclusive of the area delineated on Mr Stafford's plans. His roadway would affect the site — the ancient site where artefacts and bodies may well have been deposited over the millennia.'

'That's as may be,' Stafford sneered, 'but progress demands that we retain a balance between the past and the future. Dr Power suggests the roadway be stopped in case — and it's a very unlikely possibility — in case some other significant finds might turn up. When? Twenty years' time? Next century? Ever?' He shook his head. 'No. We can't be ruled by academics and dreamers. The people want progress. There are local jobs at risk. There's the future economic development of the valley and the surrounding area. Grouse shooting on the fells will get a boost. Amenities will be available; money will pour into the area. It's what the people, your constituents, Chairman, want.'

'Including those who are presently entrenched on Wolfcleugh Hill?' Portia Tyrrel asked, eyes ablaze with contempt.

The chairman sighed. 'Ah . . . That's another matter.' He looked at Karen Stannard. 'Are there any conclusions you would wish us to draw in this regard?' he asked.

Karen Stannard shuffled in her seat, slim fingers caressing her throat in a nervous gesture. 'I . . . we . . . I do have certain recommendations to make, Mr Chairman . . .'

But she was not at all happy in having to make them.

2

'Typical!' Portia Tyrrel stormed.

They were sitting in Arnold's car, parked on top of the fell. It had been something of an ordeal driving out here. Normally Arnold would have enjoyed the clean, fresh sea tang in the air, the views of the distant coastline and the blueness of the hills ahead of them, but Portia's annoyance had burst its bounds, even though twenty-four hours had passed since the close of the meeting in the conference room.

'I mean, what is it with her? I've been supportive, I do whatever she asks of me and if I am a bit outspoken at times, well, she ought to be grateful that I'm not just a lapdog like so many in the department!' She shot a quick, apologetic glance in Arnold's direction. 'Not that I include you in that definition, of course.'

'You've got to remember,' Arnold replied soothingly. 'She's under a lot of pressure.'

'Confirmation in her job, you mean?' Portia snorted. 'If you ask me, she's going about it the wrong way, trying to please everyone. Powell Frinton is less than impressed, that's for sure.'

She was probably right.

* * *

The arguments and the discussion had swayed back and forth, and as the meeting drew towards its close, Councillor Jonson getting edgy because he had another meeting to attend and expenses to claim, and Ken Stafford getting impatient because they seemed to be getting no nearer the solution he desired, the chief executive had turned his narrow eyes upon Karen Stannard. 'I really think it's time we obtained a recommendation from your group, Miss Stannard. It doesn't end the matter, of course, but Councillor Jonson does need something to take to his committee in due course. And within my own department there will need to be further consultation, naturally. So, what is your recommendation?'

She had been caught in a cleft stick. She was well aware that there were political figures behind Ken Stafford. She knew that Councillor Jonson, who had been wined and dined enough, wanted to be got off a hook and she was certain that Powell Frinton would be seeking some kind of scapegoat if things went wrong in the end. 'The report,' she hedged, 'was actually prepared by a member of my staff and I feel it is somewhat . . . incomplete in certain particulars. I'm not entirely happy with the thought that a firm recommendation should be made at this stage.'

Powell Frinton's ascetic, patrician features expressed a thin displeasure. He frowned, inspected the clean edge of his cuff. 'So what are you suggesting?'

'That we be given a few more days' grace. I shall instruct my staff to . . . delve a little deeper. We need firmer evidence from Dr Power and there is the matter of the protests . . .'

* * *

High on the fell, the inferences to be drawn from Karen Stannard's comments still rankled with Portia. She had fumed all the way up here as they drove towards the Cheviots, and she was still angry in spite of the spreading beauty of the landscape before them. The hazy lines of the Cheviot Hills were banked up against a summer sky, deep blue, scattered with high, wind-blown clouds. The fresh breeze lifted the heat haze. Behind them the sea beyond Amble was scudded with white horses; and ahead of them was the gentle hill, the flat edge of Wolfcleugh Moss, rising inexorably to the near skyline, the dark expanse of Wolfcleugh Woods. To the east there was a line of bold rocks standing out against the skyline, more clearly delineated than the heat-shrouded hills inland.

Arnold could have sat here and dreamed, of the people who had worked those fells, clearing and planting, grazing sheep and cattle, until the nature of the landscape changed over a thousand years and the open fells were established. He could have contemplated the dark terrors that were spoken of in Wolfcleugh Woods and the reasons why men were garrotted and hanged and buried in the swampy pools of the Moss, women interred alive there.

Instead, he was forced to concentrate on Portia as she complained bitterly about Karen Stannard and the implication that Portia had put in an incomplete report.

'I mean, suggesting there were gaps in my work! She was placing the blame on me for her own shilly-shallying! I'd warned her about the strength of feeling regarding the site; the environmental arguments were all there in the report itself. She's just hanging on until she gets a clearer line from her political friends as to what she should be recommending.'

'There is some consolation,' Arnold suggested.

'What's that?'

'Ken Stafford was mad as hell as well. He'll be charging off to pull his own strings even harder.'

Portia Tyrrel turned to look at him. Her eyes had softened somewhat, her olive skin was slightly flushed and she looked beautiful. The mingling of Scottish and Asian blood had produced intelligence — she held Oxford and Cambridge degrees — a flawless skin and a subdued, controlled beauty that fascinated Arnold. He had seen passion rise in her when she crossed swords with Karen Stannard; he had seen ancient wisdom in her eyes when she had contemplated the relationships between people she worked with, Arnold included. She was a woman of independence, resisting her father's intentions that she should go into law, heading for archaeology instead.

'Stafford. The quintessential businessman — out for profit and to hell with the consequences.' She paused, eyeing Arnold carefully, her anger subsiding as she was side-tracked. 'What did you make of that companion of his — Colm Graham?'

'A cold man.'

'Yes . . .' she agreed thoughtfully. 'Cold and controlled. You know, I read nothing in him. He barely moved, except for his eyes. I felt he could be . . . dangerous.'

Arnold thought she was probably right. However, it was irrelevant: they had been given a task by Karen Stannard — or rather, two tasks. They needed to meet Or Diane Power to discuss the work being undertaken at the Moss and they were required to investigate the situation at Wolfcleugh Woods.

He drove down the winding lanes from the fell, past frenzied scatterings of sheep, clanging his way over cattle grids until the valley opened up ahead of them, to the left the wooded area where the Shangri-La Country Park complex was planned. Distant smoke suggested some land clearing and dust hung in the air above the construction site beyond the village at Brathstone. Arnold swung left and the land began to rise as they headed towards the high mossland that was Wolfcleugh.

Diane Power was waiting for them at the site; Portia had phoned ahead saying that they needed a meeting. The muscular team leader of the Wolfcleugh Moss dig was dressed in a heavy sweater in spite of the warmth of the sun. Corduroy trousers accented her masculinity, leather boots, clay-covered, and horny hands emphasised that she was no mere academic pen-pusher. She worked with her hands on site. She gestured around her, now. 'So what do you want to know about the Moss? Three hundred years ago there were about 600 hectares of bogland here. In 1421 the right of turbary — digging of peat for fuel — was granted and it's been desecration ever since. By the 1850s there were only about 270 hectares left of the wild moss: enclosure and draining and digging had done for the rest. Hand-digging continued well into the twentieth century; it was followed by mechanical excavators in the 1970s and then more recently we've had the long trenches, the mossrooms dug in seven-metre strips by a large back-actor machine. If it hadn't been for the Wolf Man—'

She stopped, almost sheepishly, smiling at them both. 'It's easy to be seduced by tabloid shorthand, isn't it? Anyway, the digging stopped. You can see where the trucks used to come for the peat. It was stacked over there, loaded on to the waggons on that little narrow-gauge railway to the company depot, over yon side of the Moss.' She paused, her mind wandering. 'We were able to use some new facilities down at Cambridge to explore the Wolf Man remains.'

'Computed tomography?' Portia suggested.

'That's right.' There was a sudden glint of appreciation in Diane Power's brown eyes as she glanced at Portia. 'Did you know, when we used a CN scan and looked into the vault of the Wolf Man skull there was still some outer membrane, a bit of decayed brain, and you could identify part of the left eyeball and even the optic nerve.'

Portia was entranced. 'And this is the kind of thing they would destroy if they go ahead with the access road. Opportunity for further discoveries.'

Dr Power shrugged. 'Not down here, not now. But we've done some calculations. Come along with me . . .' She led the way to a small wooden hut with a roof of corrugated iron, which served as headquarters for the team who were still working on the site. Inside was a scattering of sample tables, discarded drawings, dirty coffee cups and the remains of various sandwiches. 'We don't live high here,' Dr Power intimated.

She dragged forward a rolled map and opened it, pinning its edges down with the coffee cups. 'You see, this shows the whole area of Wolfcleugh — the hill and the woods, the full extent of the ancient moss and the encroachments, modern and ancient, that have brought about such significant changes to the area. Now here's the interesting bit. These are the calculations we've made — scientific calculations, I stress, that have been drawn from trenching along this line, and higher, up here at the edge of the Wolfcleugh itself. We've been able to calculate the changes that have occurred over the last thousand years — the gradual withdrawal of the bog as the climate changed, the occasional recoveries, the impact of agriculture and natural forces on the land. Tree rings have helped, of course, and radiocarbon dating from column samples.'

'And the conclusion?'

Dr Power wrinkled her nose in distaste. 'Confirmation of our educated guesses. We already know how large the bog was in the 1400s and in the 1700s. Now, in recent centuries there's been a massive reduction. And part of the area has been reclaimed, not by Man, but by nature. In other words, the woodland on Wolfcleugh Hill has encroached upon the swamp by several hundred metres in recent times.'

Arnold looked at the map and nodded. 'I think that as a hypothesis, that's probably indisputable. But the question both Miss Stannard and the Environmental Committee will ask is, so what? Is the natural woodland of Wolfcleugh important enough to be kept sacrosanct from the depredations of big business?'

Dr Power held his glance for several seconds; she had brown, intelligent eyes. 'I believe you were at the presentation the other evening. You were near the back.'

'That's right.'

'You heard me say that I was not a supporter of ritual depositions in bogs.'

'I did.'

'I could be wrong.'

It was not often that Arnold had heard academics and theorists admit to personal uncertainty or error. Beside him, Portia looked up expectantly.

'You see, I look at it like this,' Diane Power went on. 'There are various theories: ritual deposition, selective preservation in watery places, widespread peat-cutting over the last two thousand years, industrial use in Roman times . . . but all these can be confused by the movement of water-impregnated sites subject to climatic change. Even in the mid-1980s workers here were saying that the bog was domed centrally, so we don't know how mobile this area at Wolfcleugh has been. There could have been several burst bog phenomena. So, when you put together what knowledge we have, what conflicting theories get thrown up, what do you have? Possibilities. Questions. Hypotheses. All I can say . . .'

She hesitated. Arnold waited.

Dr Power looked up towards the dark trees of Wolfcleugh Hill. 'All I can say is that I'm convinced that *if* there was a thousand-year-old tradition of bog burials and I'm not saying that this was the case — the likelihood is that for obvious reasons most of those burials would have taken place at the margins of the bog. The practical implications of trying to move bodies into the wetter areas, the more dangerous areas of the Moss, are too great. So the burials would have been at the margins. And those margins, the pools, the mud slips, the algae ponds, they would have been up there, on the edge of what is now woodland. Not here.' She muttered something to herself and shook her head. 'The Wolfcleugh Wood may be ancient, according to our ideas of age, but a large part of the present woodland was once boggy, swampy land. And the men who lived here two thousand years ago would have carried out their rituals hundreds of yards from here.' She raised her eyes reflectively. 'Up there.'

* * *

Portia wrote up her notes while Arnold took a copy of the map that had been prepared by Dr Power. She wished them luck when they left. There was no point in leaving the car where it was, so Arnold drove back to the road and took the lane that led up to the hill, some three hundred yards distant. He noted that in some areas the roadway had been widened and improved, and broad swathes had been cut in the hedgerows, in preparation for the final access route, possibly through Wolfcleugh Woods. Investment was already taking place. Ken Stafford was already spending money. No wonder he was getting so edgy.

There was a small clearing at the edge of the woods, where some cars were parked. Arnold joined them. Portia got out, leaving her clipboard behind, and eyed Arnold a little nervously. 'What sort of reception do you think we're likely to get?'

'I don't know. But I think we'll be seen as the enemy.'

The woodland seemed quiet enough but there were signs of disturbance. Scattered pieces of timber lay nearby: a damaged fence, scarred trees where bulldozers had scraped their way up towards the threatened site. There had been some road widening, the red earth raw against the scrub that was thick under the tree canopy. When Arnold raised his head he could detect woodsmoke and he heard the faint sounds of voices.

'This way.'

Portia followed as Arnold made his way down a narrow track. It wound through alder and scattered scrub, a stand of young birch and then it widened as they caught a glimpse of the road that Ken Stafford and Shangri-La Enterprises wanted widening to bring hordes of people to their entertainment complex. It was bounded by a wire fence that was still intact. Indeed, stretches of new barbed wire had been strung along vulnerable sections of the barrier. The smell of woodsmoke grew stronger and with it the odours of cooking.

'Sausages,' Portia said. 'And bacon.'

Suddenly they were at the edge of a clearing. It was a strategic point on the hill, overlooking and in direct line with the threatened roadway. Arnold could see the tactical advantage offered by the site: if the bulldozers came in to widen the road they would have to move here, up the slope, under the lee of the hill. And it was here that the stand was being made.

Arnold looked about him. Rope ladders hung from several of the trees, easily retractable, swiftly moved. Platforms had been constructed of rough-sawn timbers and between the trees at the edge of the wood ran slatted trackways, giving access to further platforms from which stones, branches and insults could be hurled. Within the canopy they could make out crude tree huts, roofed with turf and branches. The woodsmoke came from a small fire at the far edge of the clearing, where two young women were crouched, laughing among themselves. They appeared not to have noticed the presence of strangers.

There were voices deeper in the woods, vague, echoing, but clearly this was not seen as a day for confrontation. The trucks had gone, the bulldozers withdrawn after the public protests, and the game now lay in the hands of the politicians and the officials.

'Just who the hell are you?'

Arnold started, turned and he heard Portia gasp in surprise. The man standing behind him was tall, with long dark hair tied into a ponytail. He was dressed in an open-necked shirt and sweater. His jeans were worn and torn at the knee. He was well-built, muscular, with a determined mouth and his dark eyes were hard and challenging. The outdoor life had tanned his skin and his cheeks were wind-chafed. His matted beard had been trimmed from time to time, and though he might call himself a woodsman, a protector of the environment, he was also a man who took some care over his appearance. Scruffy he might be, but it was designer scruffy, Arnold thought cynically. The man carried a scuffed leather jacket in one hand and in the other a stave of ash that would easily serve as a club.

Arnold eyed the club warily. 'My name is Arnold Landon. This is Portia Tyrrel.'

'What do you want here?'

'We work for the local authority. Department of Museums and Antiquities.'

The man showed even white teeth when he grinned contemptuously. 'The last thing we want! More pen-pushers.'

'While you're a man of action, I take it?' Arnold asked evenly, somewhat nettled by the man's attitude.

'I'm doing a damn sight more than you lily-livered crawlers to protect what belongs to the people and to our heritage.' He paused, his dark eyes glittering, and drew himself up slightly. 'My name's Nick Semmens.' He clearly expected the name to mean something to them.

Portia eyed him coolly. 'You're the man the press have dubbed Tarzan.'

He inspected her critically, his eyes lingering a little too long, belying the contempt he was injecting into his tone. 'The media are there to be used and I care little if they come up with jibes like that. We know what we're doing. We know what we're campaigning for. But it's always the same, the press side with the grand battalions. They never see the reality. They never look to the future. And they're simply the lackeys of the press barons—'

'You've done this sort of thing before,' Arnold observed. 'I recognise the jargon.'

'I've fought other battles,' the man conceded. A movement beyond Arnold caught his attention and Semmens called out, 'We have company, girls. None other than the minions of the department of Museums and Antiquities, though God knows what they think they're doing here. Not helping, that's for sure.'

The two women who had been crouched at the fire were coming forward to join them. Both were in their twenties, Arnold guessed. One was dark, gypsy-looking with her black hair and tanned skin. She was dressed in a shapeless dress, all browns and greys and faded purples, and she had bound back her hair with string. She was barefoot, but there was the swing of pride in her walk that made Arnold wonder what she felt deserved that pride. Perhaps it was Nick Semmens. She linked her arm through his possessively and smiled up at him. 'What do they want?'

'To help, maybe?' The other woman was a sharp contrast to the dark girl. She was fair-haired and fair-skinned. Her nose was upturned and she had frank blue eyes. She was dressed more conventionally than her companions: a light sweater, jeans, strong walking boots. Her clothing seemed cleaner than those of Semmens and the other woman and if she spent time in these woods, Arnold doubted that she slept here. She held out her hand. 'My name's Sally Burt.'

Arnold introduced himself and Portia. 'Do I detect an Australian accent?'

She laughed in mock horror. 'That's the worst thing you can say to a New Zealander! I'm from Christchurch, South Island.'

'A long way from home.'

'Not necessarily.' She glanced in the direction of her companions and smiled. 'Don't pay too much attention to Nick and Jenny — they've developed an inbuilt hostility to any form of officialdom up here. Me, being a New Zealander, I'm more tolerant.'

Arnold laughed. 'Well, we're not up here to cause any trouble.'

'You're snooping around!' the woman called Jenny snapped. 'That usually means trouble. And you're trespassing.'

'We're not alone in that,' Portia replied a little tartly.

She stepped forward with an air of subdued belligerence. 'I know that these woods are private woods and I know that you people are well-meaning, even if your actions tend towards the violent from time to time. But the fact is, we have a job to do and from where I stand our objectives are not too far distant from yours.'

'Objectives,' Semmens sneered. 'Little Hitlers, all of you!'

'Just what are you up here for?' Sally Burt asked, sending a warning glance towards Semmens, softened, Arnold noted, with a small, conspiratorial nod. The woman called Jenny tightened her grip on Nick Semmens's arm.

Arnold looked about him as Portia explained. The area had been well planned in its defensive construction. If the bulldozers came in, the people in the trees would prevent their use. If the security men swarmed up to dislodge the inhabitants, they could use the walkways to move from tree to tree, cutting off their pursuers by a simple slicing of ropes.

He wondered just how many people would be here in Wolfcleugh Woods, defending the ancient environment. Not too many right now, perhaps, but they'd swarm back in at the first hint of trouble from Shangri-La Enterprises.

'So, you see, we're here just to help. To clarify issues. To determine whether there is a real case to be made for the protection of these woods.'

'Just because of an ancient dead body down there in Wolfcleugh Moss?' Nick Semmens jeered. 'That avoids the broader issues, denies the basic reasons for our fight. These woods have been here for a thousand years; they're an ancient, broad-leaved heritage. And they're threatened by a faceless organisation that thinks only of profit. We are here to prevent this obscenity, to face up to the hordes of—'

'No one has entered the woods yet,' Arnold interrupted coolly. 'There's no talk of any fighting, is there?'

'We're prepared for all eventualities,' Jenny said stubbornly. 'Nick and I, we're sending out a call to arms.' She had pointedly failed to mention Sally Burt, who smiled slightly.

Arnold nodded. 'I can understand that you'd want to prepare things in case a protest is really necessary, but nothing has been decided yet. The submission for planning permission has been made but not yet approved. The matter is being considered by the council—'

'If they haven't been bought off, they will be!' Semmens snapped.

'And we have yet to make a report,' Portia countered.

Semmens eyed her with open lasciviousness. 'I can guess what kind of report you'd be making. But what do you know about anything, anyway? This isn't even your country!'

At the clear reference to her Asian appearance, Portia opened her mouth to make an angry retort, but Arnold forestalled her. 'And there's still the attitude of the landowner to take into account,' he said. 'Nothing's decided yet. As you said earlier, technically we're trespassers, just like you. We haven't obtained permission of the owner to come upon this land. And neither has Shangri-La Enterprises.'

Nick Semmens sent him a glance of triumphant malignity. 'Well, that's where you're wrong, Mr Arnold Landon. You are a trespasser. We're not. We got permission for this demonstration before we set it up: these preparations are all part of a plan that involved the owner right from the start.'

Almost wearily, Sally Burt shook her head. She looked at Semmens in resignation tinged with exasperation. 'That's not strictly true, Nick, and you know it.' She looked back to Arnold and Portia. 'But as for you two being trespassers, well, maybe it would be a good idea to deal with that right now.'

She turned away, walking back down the track. 'You got your car parked down there? Follow the road up the hill. I'll meet you there. At Wolfcleugh House.'

3

The main part of the house was late seventeenth-century in construction, built in a warm red sandstone, with a Georgian pediment fronting the steps leading up into the main hall, but Arnold guessed the main house would be much older in origin. It could properly be described as a courtyard house, probably re-fashioned in the eighteenth century to a more modern style, with the courtyard roofed in to make a two-storeyed central hall with two tiers of arcades. As they came up the long metalled drive, flanked with mature oaks and beech, azalea and rhododendron, Arnold could make out to the left a stable court with a striking north range, set off with a clock tower and cupola. Arnold guessed it might have been the work of Daniel Garrett. Sally Burt was waiting for them on the front steps and Arnold wondered what right of entry a young woman from Christchurch, New Zealand might have to such an imposing old hall.

She welcomed them with a smile and an easy manner that suggested possessive rights. 'Come on in — I've warned Steven you're coming but he'll be busy in the gunroom for a little while: he has a collection of shotguns and rifles there, in spite of recent legislation. I suppose it's all been cleared with the police. Anyway, he's asked me to look after you.'

Arnold admired the fine staircase and the eighteenth-century rococo plasterwork in the saloon and the dining room, as Sally gave them a swift tour of the downstairs.

'So the owners of Wolfcleugh House used Italian *stuccatori,*' he commented.

'Is that so?' Sally enquired, staring at him somewhat wide-eyed. 'You know about such things?'

'A little. This plasterwork is mid-eighteenth-century, as is the marble fireplace . . . and the woodwork.'

She laughed a little nervously. 'In New Zealand 1901 is ancient. Anyway, what would you like to drink? The staff only come in part-time, but there's always a drinks cabinet available in the drawing room. Whisky? Brandy? Sherry?' She wrinkled her upturned nose. 'Me, I've never progressed beyond New Zealand Chardonnay, myself.'

Arnold was warming to her: she had a cheerful disposition, was unabashed by her naïveté and was trusting by nature, he guessed. He hoped suddenly that her trust might never be misplaced. He banished the dark thought as she brought him the brandy and soda he had requested. Portia settled for a glass of wine, following Sally's example.

'This drawing room is magnificent,' Arnold said, admiring the tall panelled walls, the magnificent polished oak table and the heavy brocaded furniture. The room was lit by the ceiling-high windows, which gave a vista of the meadows below and the distant line of the Cheviots above. To their right lay the dark mass of Wolfcleugh Woods, shadowed against the afternoon sky.

'So what's your connection with Wolfcleugh House?' Arnold asked curiously.

'That's a long story.' Sally Burt laughed.

'Which I'll be more than happy to relate.'

Sally turned and beamed. 'Steven! I thought you'd be longer than this. I've given our guests a drink.'

'So I see. I'll have the usual, please Sally.' He turned to Arnold and extended his hand. 'I'm Steven Burt-Ruckley.' He smiled at Portia. 'The house is graced by your presence.'

He was tall, lean and in his late forties. His hair was still dark, but the silver wings at his temples gave him an air of distinction. His nose was Roman, his eyes deep-set and lines of experience were etched around his mouth. His voice was carefully modulated, as though he weighed every word before uttering it. His handshake was courteous rather than welcoming, his manner slightly stiff, almost unworldly. Arnold gained the curious feeling that the owner of Wolfcleugh House saw himself as on a stage, moving carefully, rehearsing his lines before speaking, controlling modulation, accent, emphasis.

'I'm sorry I've been delayed — and for the slight odour of gun oil. I was busy cleaning some of my collection in the gunroom. However, my little friend was able to tell me very little about your visit,' Burt-Ruckley intoned, after he had accepted a whisky and water from Sally. 'I gather it's to do with the woods and this awful submission from Shangri-La Enterprises.' He glanced at Arnold. 'Such a dreadful name for a dreadful concept, don't you think?'

'So you don't approve of the development?' Portia asked, raising her eyebrows.

'Oh, I'm all for business and that sort of thing, and for giving the people what they want, but I can't say I'm supportive of the kind of development that's envisaged. I mean, they talk of jobs and all that but at the end of the day it will surely destroy the character of the area. There are enough Japanese and Arabs coming in at the moment, leasing shooting rights on the fells. If the Shangri-La people start using the moorland as well, heaven knows what kind of persons one might bump into on the high fell.'

It was a charade, Arnold felt: the slightly mincing tones, the patrician accent, the distant attitude, it was all part of some elaborate image that Burt-Ruckley was cultivating. He wondered where the man had come from, before he arrived at Wolfcleugh House.

Sally was laughing. 'Oh, come on, Steven, don't get up on that high horse of yours. You know that shooting rights sold to overseas visitors keep the moorlands going. Where would the grouse be, if not for the Saudis?'

'Free from gunshots, I imagine,' Portia said thoughtfully She eyed Steven Burt-Ruckley over the rim of her wine glass, her almond eyes serious, seductive and contemplative. 'So I gather you're not exactly in favour of the Shangri-La development? Why don't you stop it?'

He smiled at her, clearly a little beguiled. 'And how could I do that, Portia . . . may call you Portia?'

'Of course. But I understand you own the Wolfcleugh estates and they include the woodland abutting on to the Moss. If you don't give permission for the access road, surely that's the end of the matter. Or is it the money they might offer you?' she added teasingly.

Burt-Ruckley's smile was genuine. 'The money hardly comes into it. I might have started life in poor circumstances, but things changed when I married. This house is well maintained because I can afford it, thanks to my dear wife, sadly no longer with us. No, I don't approve of the scheme, but . . .' His mouth grew serious, pinched slightly at the corners. 'I did talk to my lawyers, but it seems there are certain complications. There is a right of way that runs along the edge of the woods, largely where the new road would be constructed. And . . .' He sighed theatrically. 'There's always the shadow of compulsory purchase. I'm told it is within the power of the authorities to act in that depressing manner.'

'Don't you have friends in the county?' Arnold asked carefully. 'Friends who might be able to help, exert a little influence?'

He thought he detected a note of asperity in Burt-Ruckley's reply. 'I've never got much involved with the county set. And I certainly wouldn't go cap in hand to them.'

Portia sipped her drink thoughtfully. 'So are you opposing the scheme?'

Burt-Ruckley shrugged diffidently. 'I suppose I am, at a distance. I'm not what you might call an activist at all. I've never been what you might describe as a joiner. I enjoy a peaceful life, here at Wolfcleugh. I've given permission to that unwashed lot that Sally seems so fond of to play their games, build tree houses and all that sort of thing, against the day the big battalions might be brought up to the front. But I don't really want to be involved at all. It's so tiresome.'

He glanced at Arnold as he spoke and something moved deep in his eyes, a nervous tension. Somehow Arnold felt that Burt-Ruckley was perhaps more concerned about the Shangri-La development than he was prepared to admit.

They chatted on in a desultory fashion for a little while longer. Sally asked Burt-Ruckley for permission for the department of Museums and Antiquities to visit the site as and when they saw fit and he gave that permission graciously. When he had finished his own drink he left them.

Sally saw them off the premises. They stood on the steps in the late afternoon sunlight, looking about them at the sloping meadows and the distant stream, the long, curving drive flanked with shrubs and trees, the rise to the hill and the ancient woods.

Portia sighed. 'It's so beautiful here.'

Sally nodded, smiling. 'It certainly is. Not that we can't match this kind of countryside in South Island.' Arnold glanced at her. 'Burt-Ruckley said he could explain your presence, but we never got around to it.'

Sally laughed, crinkling her nose. 'Well, I'm *sort* of family, in a distant kind of way. I was born and brought up in New Zealand, and I heard vague stories about Northumberland, but I didn't listen too much, you know how it is? And then when my parents died it was sort of too late. We always leave it too late to ask questions of the people who know, don't we? Still, when I finally decided to go for my Master's I plumped for Newcastle University, chance to get back to my roots, you know? And when I'd settled in, I began to check out what little I recalled about my mother's background. She was a Burt-Ruckley, you see.'

'So you're directly related to the owner of Wolfcleugh.'

Sally scratched at her cheek and squinted thoughtfully into the sun. 'Well, sort of. It's all a bit complicated, I guess.

My mother was half-sister, apparently, to Amanda Burt-Ruckley. She emigrated and more or less lost touch. Amanda married, down south somewhere, in London—'

'Not here at Wolfcleugh?' Portia asked in surprise.

'No, she wasn't living here then.' Sally shook her head. 'This was in the early eighties, or late seventies or whatever. She was working for an advertising agency, apparently, in London, when she met Steven and they married. It was some time after that she heard the owner of Wolfcleugh had died and she came into the inheritance.'

'Quite an inheritance,' Portia murmured.

Sally grinned. 'Yeah. Good, innit!'

They both laughed, giggling like schoolgirls. 'Anyway,' Sally continued, 'there I was at Newcastle, doing my thing and wondering about my family, so I decided to look up the Burt-Ruckleys. I met Steven and he was very welcoming. He invited me to come and stay whenever I wanted. He lives a pretty lonely life. So I come up here from time to time, and then when all this trouble started I went down and talked with the protesters in the woods, got to know them. They're all right, really. Nick, for all his bluster is rather sweet.'

Arnold nodded, unconvinced. 'So Steven Burt-Ruckley . . . did you say he was married to Amanda Burt-Ruckley? But his name—'

Sally grinned. 'That's right. Confusing isn't it? No, Steven isn't a blood relative of mine. He's related only by marriage. You see, he married Amanda down south and she became Mrs Palmer, but when she came into possession of Wolfcleugh they agreed he should change his surname, so she could revert to the family name. Sort of carrying on tradition. Things like that are important to people who hold landed property, isn't that so? Not that it makes much difference in the long run.'

'How do you mean?'

Sally shrugged. 'Well the name will die with Steven, won't it? Two years after they moved up here and Steven changed his name, Amanda was killed. Show jumping, I believe. Broke her neck. She and Steven hadn't had any children. So there it will end.'

'Does that mean you might come into the inheritance eventually?' Portia asked in mock excitement.

Sally giggled again. 'A very remote thought! No, I'm pretty sure I won't be involved. Steven will do with Wolfcleugh what he wills — and I believe he has some ideas . . .'

CHAPTER TWO

1

Arnold had a number of files to deal with during the next few days. They took him out of the office, which was always pleasant since he could then avoid the tensions that were now apparent between Karen Stannard and Portia, and the gossip that tended to swirl around whenever staff caught a whiff of dispute.

He spent a few days in the company of an earnest young man who had been given a grant to complete a monograph on industrial archaeology. Drafted in as an adviser, chauffeur and general wet-nurse, Arnold quite enjoyed driving around the north-east, explaining how the landed families in County Durham and Northumberland had taken the initiative in exploiting local resources, supplying capital for mining and transport, building staithes, extending rail networks. He showed his companion Seaton Sluice, built by the Delavals, and Seaham Harbour, constructed by Lord Londonderry.

It was with a certain reluctance that he returned to the office. He was not there long before he was summoned to the presence.

Karen Stannard seemed calm and controlled, but there were high spots of colour in her cheeks. She invited him to sit down and then for a little while ignored him, staring out of the window thoughtfully. Arnold was aware that Portia had been in to see her earlier: information travelled rapidly in the office. He guessed it would be something to do with that meeting.

Karen Stannard swivelled in her chair. The sunlight glinted in her hair. As always her eyes were of an indeterminate colour, their expression on this occasion suspicious. 'So what's your view about the Shangri-La situation, Arnold?'

'I'm not sure things have moved forward very much,' he replied carefully.

She raised an elegant eyebrow. 'Then you must be out of touch. To begin with, Councillor Jonson is making impatient noises. Powell Frinton called me in to his office yesterday, and he tells me there is a ground swell of opinion among the councillors that this thing is dragging on too long. They want a decision to be made.'

'I imagine that'll be Ken Stafford putting on the pressure.'

She regarded him with faint displeasure. 'You don't like him.'

'That's irrelevant.' Arnold shrugged. 'I think the value of his scheme to the valley is overestimated. I can't make a judgement of it as a commercial venture. But none of that matters. The politicians will have a view.'

'As will the protesters. Have you seen the local newspapers on the matter?' When Arnold shook his head, she went on, 'There's all the signs of a campaign against Shangri-La. It's good news for their circulation, of course, when trouble gets stirred up. But there's been a long interview with a young man called Semmens—'

'I've met him.'

'And?'

Arnold shrugged again. 'An arrogant young man. A regular protester. He has views. And some support from the landowner of Wolfcleugh, Mr Burt-Ruckley — though that gentleman doesn't want to get too much involved, it seems. Semmens claims he can gather protesters and certainly a number of people have been working in those woods, erecting tree houses, walkways, that sort of thing.'

'If push comes to shove, will there be a battle?'

'Is the decision about to be made, then?'

Her eyes seemed to have a violet shade now, the line of her mouth was inviting. Arnold shook his head slightly: he could never quite make up his mind about Karen Stannard. She regarded him speculatively, confidentiality in her tone when she said, 'I think I know which way things should be going. Like it or not, Arnold, we live in a political world. And we have to look out for ourselves. The pressures are building up Stafford, Jonson, Powell Frinton and the members of the council who are just waiting for our report so they can use it as an excuse, wave it at the protesters and the newspapers. Say it all makes sense.'

'So?'

'So, on balance, I don't think we can resist the forces of progress.'

'Diane Power won't be pleased,' Arnold suggested. 'Neither will Portia Tyrrel.' There was a short silence.

'How do you feel she's settled in at the department, Arnold?'

'Well enough.' He could guess what was coming.

'I'm not so sure.' She sighed. 'I'm beginning to feel maybe I made a mistake, appointing her. She's quick, able and intelligent, but she tends to go somewhat off the rails from time to time. And she can be capable of a certain . . . stubbornness, which spills over into disobedience.'

Arnold was silent. Karen Stannard did not like that: she looked at him gloomily. 'I see you as an ally, Arnold, you know that.'

It was far from the truth, but he let her carry on without contradiction.

'I'm worried about Portia. You see, she doesn't understand the danger we're in. Politically, I mean. If we put in a biased report it could bring about all sorts of repercussions. Cuts in our funding. Non-replacement of personnel. Change of attitude in the council . . .'

Non-confirmation of her promotion, Arnold thought cynically.

'I've talked to her, of course. But I'm a woman and sometimes, with two women, it can get in the way, you know?' She eyed him, injecting sincerity into her tone. 'She likes you, Arnold, I know that. She respects you. I think if you were to talk to her she might listen.'

'And what should I be saying to her?' Arnold asked non-committally.

Karen Stannard was not misled by the innocence in his tone. She kept the suspicion out of her own voice and lidded her eyes seductively. 'As I said, I have now put the finishing touches to the departmental report. It will soon be submitted. It suggests there is no departmental objections we can raise, no case against the building of the access road. I talked to Portia about it. She disagrees. She wants us to call for a scheduling of the wood as a protected area. She wants us to support Diane Power. She wants the council to enter into an agreement with Mr Burt-Ruckley which will close off the opportunity to Shangri-La. She wants a compulsory purchase order . . . she wants all sorts of things, Arnold. And she claims she's found some more compelling information to support her arguments.'

Karen Stannard leaned forward, elbows on her desk, hands knuckled under her chin. Her green eyes held his. 'She's even had the temerity to invite Burt-Ruckley into the office for a discussion. Without my knowledge. He arrives at two this afternoon. I've no intention of giving the meeting the status it hardly deserves by attending in person.'

'You want me to sit in.'

'And report back. I want this thing headed off Arnold. It's important to the department that things don't get out of hand. Important to the department, to me and to you.' She smiled vaguely. 'And to our headstrong young Portia also, of course.'

* * *

43

Steven Burt-Ruckley sat stiffly in the chair that had been placed in front of the desk in Portia's office. When Arnold tapped on the door and walked in, Portia looked up in surprise. She had been writing something in a notebook when he entered, but he gained the impression that she had had little opportunity to proceed deeply into the discussion with Burt-Ruckley. The man nodded coolly in response to Arnold's greeting.

'Can I help you, Arnold?' Portia asked in a suspicious tone.

'Karen thought it would be useful if I sat in on the discussion,' he replied flatly. They looked at each other for several seconds and for a moment he thought Portia's temper was going to explode. Then she relaxed slightly: there was a message in her eyes. She knew he was not Karen Stannard's lackey. She trusted him to maintain a fair balance.

'I'm grateful that you found time to call in to see me,' Portia said, turning in her chair, smiling winningly at Burt-Ruckley.

'It's my pleasure. I had some business to transact in Morpeth anyway. But I wasn't very clear about the reason for the meeting.'

'Inevitably, it concerns the proposed roadway at the edge of Wolfcleugh,' she explained. 'From our meeting at your house, and after talking with Sally, I gather that you are opposed to the building of the access road.'

Burt-Ruckley's eyes were hesitant. 'As a matter of principle, yes.'

'And you support the protest to try to prevent the construction.'

'Once again, in principle.' Burt-Ruckley's lips were thin and dry, his glance calmer now. 'I cannot say I'm entirely happy at the presence of the protesters on my land, but if it serves to prevent a greater evil, I feel I must accommodate their wishes.'

'There could be a battle,' Portia suggested, glancing at Arnold as though for support. 'And it will be a battle Tarzan Semmens and his crew can't win.'

'Is that what they call him?' Burt-Ruckley's mouth broadened in a reluctant smile. 'Why should they not win? A public protest—'

'Will fail, because there's too much money involved. Ken Stafford and Shangri-La are pulling out all the stops. They're calling in favours and they're putting pressure on the politicians to approve the plans. It's all going to happen, Mr Burt-Ruckley, and a gang of tree-hopping protesters can't stop it.'

He was silent for a little while, eyes lidded. 'So why are you telling me this?'

Portia drew a deep breath. 'Because I think there is a way it can be stopped.'

'Involving me.'

'You're the landowner. In a sense it all comes down to you. I know you've been advised that there is a right of way across the edge of the woods. I am aware your lawyers tell you the county could slap a compulsory purchase order on you to force things through. But they won't dare take that step, not without an enquiry and that would mean a government inspector and a protracted period of investigation. Something Ken Stafford wouldn't want.'

'So how do you feel I can help?'

Portia hesitated, glanced at the notes she had been making in her leather-bound notebook. 'I've been in discussion with the librarian at Newcastle University. She thinks she's found something which would be of interest and which we could use in our campaign.'

Burt-Ruckley's eyes glinted with suspicion.

'To get Wolfcleugh Woods designated as a special site for archaeological research.'

There was a short silence. Arnold watched Burt-Ruckley closely. The man seemed uneasy, wary. He shifted awkwardly in his chair. 'What exactly would that entail?' Burt-Ruckley asked.

'Diane Power, who heads up the team investigating Wolfcleugh Moss, is convinced that there may well be further discoveries to be made in the area that ShangriLa want to use for road building. I think I might have come across evidence to support her claim that the swamp extended into the wooded area only three hundred years ago. All she needs is your permission, your support . . . and some funding.'

'You want me to give money to her project?'

'If you can match the grants she expects to get from Europe—' Portia began eagerly.

He held up a hand. It was quivering slightly. 'Money is hardly a problem, as I said before. But you seem to be suggesting an extension of the exploration of the Moss into Wolfcleugh Woods.'

'It would be no great disturbance,' Portia insisted. 'The work would not start immediately — and once it did start, it would continue over a period of years. But at least it would stir public and government opinion to oppose Ken Stafford's scheme; even delay would help, because delay would probably kill off Shangri-La's interest anyway . . .'

Her voice died away as she recognised the doubt in Burt-Ruckley's eyes. He glanced at Arnold. Slowly, he shook his head. 'I think you misunderstand my position, Miss Tyrrel. Wolfcleugh Woods belong to me. They are ancient; they are part of our heritage; I want them left as they are. I don't want people tramping around there. I permit those hooligans to build in the trees simply because I see them as a lesser evil. Once the threat of the Shangri-La development is past, I will insist they leave. I will use them as far as I can to resist Shangri-La, as I will resist a compulsory purchase order or anything of that kind. But I am a passive resister only. I do not wish to get involved.'

'But allowing the archaeological team in would help the case!'

'You still miss the point.' Burt-Ruckley's eyes were suddenly hard. 'They are my woods. I don't want Shangri-La in them. I don't want the protesters in them. And I don't want Dr Power and her archaeology team in them either. There has to be another way.'

'If there is, Mr Burt-Ruckley,' Portia said grimly, slumping back in her chair, 'then you'll have to come up with it.'

* * *

'I thought he'd have jumped at the chance to support the idea,' Portia exclaimed angrily as Arnold drove her south to Newcastle.

Arnold also was intrigued by the man's seeming ambivalence, but he said nothing. He sensed there was something behind Burt-Ruckley's reluctance, other than money, and it might be that Sally Burt would know something about it.

The stubbornness displayed by Burt-Ruckley had annoyed Portia. Indeed, it was perhaps that annoyance that had led her to suggest Arnold might drive her to meet the librarian in Newcastle. She wanted to let off steam to someone. As for the appointment, it was not one she had mentioned to Karen Stannard and she had hoped to keep it after getting support from Burt-Ruckley. Now, she felt the meeting was even more important, in view of Burt-Ruckley's refusal to offer support. 'He just wants a quiet life,' she snarled to Arnold, 'but without our help he's going to get caught up in a hell of a lot of trouble. And he's too stubborn or too lazy to see it.'

Arnold parked near the Town Moor and they made their way in the early evening sun down past the university lodgings until they came to the library building itself. They were greeted at the library reception desk by Georgina Hope, a deputy librarian who specialised in historical manuscripts in her lectures to the history department. She was small, earnest and middle-aged. Her spectacles gave her an owlish appearance and an air of wisdom. She seemed entranced by Portia and was very quick to assure them of any assistance they might require. 'As it happens, there seems to be a resurgence of interest in Wolfcleugh. One of our students has been doing some research on it.'

'Really?' Portia remarked politely.

'That's right. A Miss Burt. She has some connection with the owner of Wolfcleugh House and she's been researching her family, that sort of thing.'

'Sally Burt,' Arnold said. 'Yes, we know her. From New Zealand.'

'That's right. I thought her accent was Australian,' the librarian mused. 'Do you know her well? I mean, do you see her often?'

'Not really.'

'Oh. It's just that she hasn't been in for a while and someone called here to see her the other day. What was his name . . . ? Dickson, I think. He seemed rather . . . odd. He asked me . . . well anyway, if you see her tell her this man was looking for her. Now then,' she said, leading the way into a quiet seminar room off the main library, 'as for your own request, rather more interesting than genealogy I must say, I started searching, first for any reference to Wolfcleugh Moss, or the woods themselves. As it happened there is a considerable amount of documentation regarding both, but it is mainly of a mythical or legendary nature.'

'Tall stories to frighten the children?' Arnold asked.

'Something like that. In the nineteenth century there were a number of publications in the north-east which concentrated on local stories, some historical, some legendary. There is one, *Legends of the Northumberland Hinterland*, which contains quite a number of stories about Wolfcleugh. A completely erroneous discussion of how the name came into being: the legend of the dreaded and rapacious northern werewolf reputed to live on the hill, unauthenticated stories of ghostly lights at night, ritual burials from Viking times, night-stalkers, all the usual sort of thing. There is also a short series in 1872 regarding the Moss itself and ritual decapitation. It's from that article, really, that I got the first hint of an older source.'

'How do you mean?' Portia asked.

'Well, most of these stories are simply that — stories, which are based on rumour or gossip, or which are, literally, fiction. But the series of articles on the Moss seemed to bear a different ring and after some research into the author I was able to discover that he did indeed have some older provenance for his accounts.'

'How much older?' Arnold enquired.

Georgina Hope gestured them each to take a seat at the table, where she had earlier placed some thick, leather-bound volumes. 'Everything now is put on microfiche or microdot or whatever it's called,' she fussed, 'but I much prefer to use the original material where I can find it. These volumes were actually gathering dust at our centre in Byker, where nobody ever goes. Imagine! But I just love the smell of the dust and the feel of the heavy paper . . . and I can't read those microfilms anyway. It's in here I found the name. The Reverend Mr Hatch.'

She slipped her fingers into the book where she had marked a place with a slip of paper and heaved the volume open. It fell with a thud on the table and dust danced in the air. Portia coughed. Arnold leaned forward. 'The Reverend Hatch. An antiquarian?'

'They often were, weren't they, those clergymen?' Georgina squealed in a pleased tone. 'There they were, tramping their parishes, ministering to their flocks, writing their resounding sermons taking sides in the great religious debates of the day, and in their spare hours reading and looking and digging. They often got it wrong,' she averred, shaking her head, 'but at least they were interested.'

'And why should we be interested in the Reverend Hatch?' Portia asked, a hint of impatience creeping into her tone.

Georgina Hope seemed not to have detected the impatience. She smiled in a curiously secretive way. 'I think you will be, because he had the living at St Edmund's parish, just over the hill from Wolfcleugh. Indeed, he knew the area well. But I'll come back to that. The first important thing I have to tell you is that in 1632 a man and a woman died in the Moss, from exposure. It was a winter night and they were lost at the edge of the mire. It was several months before they were discovered, frozen in a snowdrift. They were buried on the spot, without benefit of church. And it seems they were buried in the peat bog.'

'Why without benefit of a church blessing?' Portia asked curiously.

Georgina Hope shrugged her thin shoulders. 'I don't know. Local prejudice of some kind. Maybe they were gypsies.'

'Or lovers caught in adultery,' Arnold suggested. He caught Portia's glance and the rolling of her eyes. He smiled.

Georgina Hope sniffed. 'Whatever the reason,' she went on, 'there they remained for thirty years. Until our Reverend Mr Hatch came along. And left us an account. The original is a little difficult to make out, because of the archaic language, but a friend of mine in the department has made out a fair copy in modern prose style.' She slipped a sheet of paper from the book and placed it in front of them.

Arnold read it with interest.

. . . some of the countrymen, having observed the extraordinary quality of the soil in preserving dead bodies from corruption, were curious enough to open the ground where these people were reputed to have been interred. They wished to see if these persons had been so preserved. They found them in no way altered. They were after exposed for sight over twenty years although they were much changed in that time. The woman, by some rude people had been taken from the ground, to which one might impute her greater decay . . .

There was a short silence. Portia grimaced. 'So your star-crossed lovers, if that's what they were, ended up as a sort of sideshow for local people to gawp at.'

Georgina Hope nodded. 'It was all rather macabre, I imagine. It ended when the local squire from Wolfcleugh paid for a proper funeral at St Edmund's.'

Arnold was thoughtful. He could see the relevance of the discovery, but it was hardly enough to persuade opponents of an extension of Wolfcleugh Moss investigations. 'The Reverend Hatch . . . did he make any other references to the bog?'

Georgina Hope smiled and threw a proud, triumphant glance in Portia's direction. 'He did indeed. In fact, he drew upon various sources available to him, but now lost to us, to prepare a map of a series of bog finds, some artefacts, some mummified remains, that had been obtained by peat diggers over the years.'

'He mapped their locations?'

'With some deliberation.'

'How many were there?' Arnold asked.

'Twenty-two,' Georgina Hope replied in quiet satisfaction.

'Things are beginning to look up,' Portia muttered.

'There's more,' the librarian asserted. 'I said earlier that the Reverend Hatch knew the area well. In fact, apart from his mapping of the finds — which, of course, we can only accept in face of a lack of primary sources — he also produced a map of the parish. With some precision.'

'So?'

'It includes Wolfcleugh Hill, the woods and Wolfcleugh Moss. Dated 1674. It's here . . .' She produced a photocopy of the original, which was probably lying in some safer place, Arnold concluded.

He stared at it, tracing the lines, the cottages and farms named, the church boundaries. A slow excitement stirred in his veins. Supplemented by tithe maps and other parish references they would be able to identify exactly the boundary of the Moss as drawn in 1647 by the Reverend Hatch. But even without reference to such information he could already see the implications. He placed his forefinger on the map, pointing. 'Look. The edge of the bog, delineated with representations of tufts of grass, rushes and water. And the edge of Wolfcleugh Wood. Now look along here to Girbal Cottage and Manor Farm . . .'

'The discovery of the two bodies,' Portia breathed, 'the location is right at the edge of the woods.'

'And the line of the woods is way back from its present position,' Arnold said.

'Miss Hope, I could kiss you!' Portia exclaimed and did so.

Arnold contented himself by shaking the librarian's hand. But he did wonder what it might be like to be kissed by Portia Tyrrel.

2

After the piecemeal development of the Georgian period when new squares and terraces had mushroomed to celebrate the end of the Border hostilities, bold and imaginative planning in the nineteenth century had created a new town of Newcastle, one of elegant wide streets lined with classical frontages and grand municipal buildings. If Arnold did not approve of the changes made later in the twentieth century, the destruction of Eldon Square to build a massive shopping complex, he nonetheless liked the city for the glimpses it still gave of its mediaeval heart, corners of Tudor and Georgian origin, a twelfth-century keep built by Henry II and one of the most majestic streets in Europe named after Lord Grey.

He liked the Northumberland Arms also. Located near the commercial centre of the city, within walking distance of the university, it was a no-nonsense sort of place. It still had a creaking wooden floor, dark-stained and uneven, and a long bar with an old-fashioned brass rail. The seating in the bar bore a greater resemblance to church pews than was accidental: he suspected they had started life in that way. And the lounge which led off from the side street was somewhat shabby, but proud of it. Sporting prints on the wall hung side by side with spy cartoons — perhaps the gift of a grateful

53

Victorian lawyer on his deathbed. The Northumberland Arms seemed to have attracted a number of such eccentric bequests: a rusty suit of armour built in 1920 rather than 1420, a stuffed parrot with moulting feathers, gift of some Dutch sea captain who had plied the Tyne in his later years; a fake chastity belt built of iron with a projecting spike. University students were prone to try to steal it, for what purposes Arnold was loath to consider.

'Is this one of your favourite haunts?' Portia asked, smiling as they entered the lounge.

'I'm rarely in Newcastle,' Arnold prevaricated. 'But I think the place is fun. What will you have to drink?'

'In the excitement of the moment,' Portia replied, hugging to herself the brown envelope in which the librarian had placed the statement and maps of the Reverend Hatch, 'I'll celebrate with a large glass of white wine.'

'Coming up.'

Arnold had suggested they might stop off for a drink and then have a meal together, rather than drive back to Morpeth immediately. She had accepted with alacrity. There was a light in her eyes as they left the library and walked along towards the city centre. Now, as he brought her the white wine along with a brandy and soda for himself, she looked up at him, took the glass, raised it, sipped it and asked, 'So, Arnold, is this a date?'

He caught the twinkle in her eye and shook his head. 'No, a professional conference over drinks and dinner. You seemed pretty high back in the library — I thought it would be a pity to let it drain out of you in the drive back to Morpeth. You looked as though you wanted to celebrate.'

'Don't you?'

He hesitated, considering the matter. 'I don't know. Maybe I'm more cautious, temperamentally, than you. I'll agree that the information we now have will be useful to Dr Power in making her case, but she is still facing the big guns.' He sipped his brandy and watched her animated features for a moment, noting the glow in her olive skin, the sparkle in her eyes. 'Just what do you intend doing with this information?'

'I shall give it to Dr Power, of course, to help her make a case for an extension of the search site. And I shall make out a minority report, disagreeing with the findings presented by Karen Stannard.'

'Your boss.'

'So?'

'Could cost you your job. At the very least, give rise to hostility between you. Is it worth it?'

'Worth fighting for, you mean?' She shook her head. 'Karen Stannard's going to do what she thinks the politicians want and the big money people want. She's lacking in integrity. She should be supporting Dr Power, not giving in to the pressure. I've already had some of this out with her, though maybe in not such plain language, and she wasn't pleased. Not least because I think a year or so ago she might have thought the same way I do. But she's been corrupted. By fear. By compromise. By an overwhelming desire to be confirmed as director of the department.'

Arnold ducked his head doubtfully. 'Don't overplay your hand, Portia. The issues aren't so clear-cut as you think. As for Karen Stannard, I'm not sure you're right about her integrity—'

'What is it with you and her, Arnold?' she asked suddenly.

He was caught off guard. 'What do you mean?'

She regarded him steadily, her eyes dark and knowing. 'I've been around for almost a year now. I've watched you both. I can't make it out. You kind of circle each other, you know? You go your own way, hold to your own principles and arguments, and maybe she agrees with you, maybe she doesn't. But she's wary of you and you of her. But why is that? Have you crossed her so she doesn't trust you?'

Arnold managed an uneasy laugh. 'There's something of that,' he admitted.

'But there's more than that, too. I think there's some kind of spark that neither of you is prepared to admit to.

From time to time I've got to wondering what would happen if . . . Ho, ho, ho, what do we have here?'

Her glance had slid past Arnold as she was talking. He turned his head, following her line of sight. There was someone at the bar he recognised: tanned features, ponytail, designer beard. Nick Semmens, laughing, buying drinks. Then he leaned back slightly and Arnold caught sight of his companion. She was gesturing, clearly suggesting they should take a seat on one of the pews in the main bar. It was Sally Burt.

'So, all sorts of non-dates tonight, then,' Portia suggested, smiling.

'How do you mean?'

'Well, I can't imagine young Jenny back at Wolfcleugh Woods would be too happy at the thought of her boyfriend chumming up with our Sally here in Newcastle.' She caught the doubtful look on his face and giggled. 'Aw, come on, Arnold, you must have recognised what was going on between Tarzan and his Jenny! They wouldn't have been spending time up among those trees eating bananas, you know!'

Arnold grinned. 'They did seem pretty close. But I also got the impression that Sally was rather friendly towards Semmens.'

'Mm.' Portia sipped her drink. 'She needs to be careful there. I don't think that guy is good news. Trouble will follow him. Anyway, let's have another look at this map. Do you think we can get hold of the tithe maps for the period to make the necessary comparisons?'

Grateful that the topic of conversation had changed, Arnold pored over the maps developed by the Reverend Hatch. Their heads were close together and he caught the sweet smell of the wine on her breath. The scent of her skin affected him too and he found some difficulty in concentrating.

They were still huddled over the documents when Arnold finished his drink. 'I think we have time for another before we go and get something to eat.'

'Where do you have in mind?' she asked.

'There are several places we can take a look at the lower end of Grey Street, above the Side. I'll give you the choice: Italian, French, Portuguese—'

'Chinese?' she asked mischievously.

He laughed. 'If you like. Nothing more to drink for you?'

She shook her dark head and he rose, headed for the bar. As he did so he heard the sound of breaking glass and raised voices. When he reached the bar he could see into the other room. There were two men there, squaring up to each other. A table had crashed over, a chair sent spinning. Huddled in the corner, against the wall, scared, was Sally Burt. And one of the two belligerent men was Nick Semmens. Arnold put down his glass and headed for the door into the other room. As he went, he called out to Portia, 'Stay where you are!'

He was already too late when he entered. The two men had leapt at each other and were struggling, arms locked around each other's neck swaying and panting in a furious struggle. Another table went over and Arnold heard the bar-man shouting for order, above a rising crescendo of voices, some cheering the men on. Near the door there was a general scramble as a group of young people, not relishing being involved at the fringe of a stand-up fight, headed for the exit. No attempt was being made to intervene and Arnold was disinclined to take any part himself. It was Sally Burt he was concerned with. She was huddled against the wall, scared, panicky.

The two men swayed and stamped, and Arnold could not get past them. It was not particularly serious or danger-ous as a fight: it was more of a wrestling match than anything else. Then, as Nick Semmens tried to bring his knee up into the older man's groin, everything turned ugly.

The older man broke free. He was perhaps in his mid-forties; short-cropped hair, greying at the temples with a stocky, muscular body that suggested hard manual labour. He was at least twenty years older than Semmens but he was not breathing as hard as the younger man: he was fitter and he was stronger, but there was a mad gleam in his eyes now and Arnold realised he was out for blood. Semmens was taunting him, foolishly. 'Come on, old man! Show me you're not all mouth!'

The older man took a deep, angry breath. Then, quite deliberately he turned away, walked across to the bar and picked up a pint mug half full of beer. He threw the liquid aside, smashed the beer glass on the brass rail below the bar and grinned viciously. His temper was not under control, but had been channelled into intent. 'I'm going to grind this into your bloody face,' he snarled. 'You won't be such a pretty boy with the girls then, will you?'

Nick Semmens stood his ground for one long moment and then the jeering confidence began to drain away from him as the other advanced. He backed away, stumbling as he collided with a chair. He picked it up, threw it in his opponent's direction and the barman was bawling, shouting raucously behind the bar, calling for an end to the confrontation. More glass shattered as someone got out of the way, knocking over some bottles.

The older man extended his left hand, beckoning, jeering, with the light of murder in his eyes. 'Come on, fancy man. Let's see the colour of your blood.'

Arnold had no intention of getting involved at this dangerous stage. His objective was to drag Sally Burt out of range of the conflict. He saw his chance and acted swiftly. He stepped past the two antagonists and crossed the room quickly. He grabbed Sally by the wrist. She seemed almost in a daze: her terrified features turned up to his, he saw recognition in her eyes and then he was dragging her towards the doorway that led back into the lounge.

The movement changed patterns of violence. The man with the beer glass caught the movement out of the corner of his eye and swung round, uncertain whether he was being attacked from behind. He started to shout something when he saw Arnold dragging the girl with him, but in his moment of distraction Nick Semmens seized his own chance. He grabbed another chair, drove forward with it, slamming one leg into the stomach of the man with the beer glass. He went down on his knees, gasping, still holding the glass and the last glimpse Arnold had of the conflict as he pushed Sally through the doorway into the lounge was of Semmens swinging the chair at the head of the man on the floor.

The door crashed behind Arnold and pandemonium broke out in the general bar.

'What the hell is going on in there?' Portia gasped as she saw Sally, distraught, half crying in terror. She reached out for her, drew her down to the seat beside her, extended a protective arm. The rest of the people in the lounge were already crowded forward, looking through to the general area at the progress of the battle there.

'It's Nick Semmens,' Arnold said shortly.

'Is he all right?' Sally asked in sudden alarm.

'He's holding his own,' Arnold said grimly, 'but both of them want locking up.'

It was almost as though a wish was fulfilled in part, because even as he said the words a shout went up in the street outside 'Make way for the polis!'

The cavalry had arrived.

There was a continuation of noise in the bar room but gradually it subsided. Sally was shivering and Portia had her arm around her. 'What was it all about?'

'I don't know, really,' Sally replied. 'Nick was in town and he called me, asked me if I'd like to have a drink with him. I was at a loose end and I knew this pub . . . a lot of the students come here . . .'

'We saw you at the bar,' Arnold said. 'You came in shortly after us.'

'Well, I'd taken a seat and Nick joined me, and we were sort of just chatting there for a while, and then this man came in. He stood inside the entrance of the bar for a while, staring at us. I got the impression he had come in looking for Nick. And then he just came over and swore at Nick. He was looking for a fight, even then, I think.'

'Nick knew him, then.'

'It seems so. But then everything happened so quickly.' She shuddered. 'That man, he just said "Get rid of your whore" and Nick stood up and swung a punch at him, and the next moment they were struggling in the centre of the room. At first I even thought it was a joke, play-acting, horsing about, you know what I mean? And then glasses and tables went flying, and people started running out of the pub and I was trapped in the corner, unable to get away from it. Then he grabbed that beer glass and that's when I really got scared . . .'

'All right,' Arnold soothed. 'I think it's about all over now. I'll get you a drink, help to calm you down.'

He went up to the bar.

The bartender was flushed, polishing a glass in brisk anger as he watched what was going on. 'Mad buggers,' he muttered as Arnold came up. Arnold glanced through. There was no sign of Nick Semmens but two police officers were talking to the man who had picked up the beer glass. He was seated, truculent, shaking his head. As they watched a third police officer came in, waved and the man was dragged to his feet. 'Want locking away, those mad bastards who can't hold their temper. Still, seen worse on a Saturday night when Chelsea's in town. That's when it can really get rough. What'll you have, bonny lad?'

Arnold bought a whisky and took it back to the table where Portia was still sitting with her arm round Sally. 'You'll feel better if you get some of this inside you,' Arnold assured her.

She made a face as the harsh liquor caught her throat, but she sipped at it, looking miserable. 'What's going on now?' she whispered.

'I think they've carted away both the idiots,' Arnold suggested.

'What'll happen to Nick?'

'At the least he'll cool off in the cells, I imagine. Or maybe even get off with a warning. You don't know what it was all about?'

She shook her head. 'That man came in looking for trouble.'

The door from the main bar opened and one the police constables Arnold had seen looked in. He grunted and came across to them. He nodded to Arnold and asked Sally if she was all right. Sally nodded.

'I was told you was in here, Miss. You was with one of those two, hey?'

She nodded again. 'And that would be?'

'Nick Semmens.'

'Like to tell me what it was all about?'

She explained she had no idea, that the other man had come in looking for trouble, had started the fight and she hadn't a clue who he was.

'Aye, well, we know the lad right enough. When he's had a few he's been known to sling a few punches. Though it's been a fair while now since he's cut up rough around town. I heard he'd calmed down since he started his little business. Doing pretty well, I heard. Still, a night in the cooler will calm him down. Up to the sarge to decide after that.'

'You say you know him?' Arnold asked curiously.

'Oh, aye. Lad by the name of Farley, Joe Farley. Used to be a bit of a tearaway, but last few years sobered up, running a canny little business, hiring out earth-shifting equipment, like. Anyway, if you're all right, Miss, and you've nothin' to add, I'll leave you with your friends. No point in draggin' you into this business, is there, if there's no need?' He nodded, smiled and touched his cap.

After he had gone, Sally sipped again at the whisky.

She still seemed shaken by the events. Arnold leaned towards her. 'Are you sure you're all right?'

She nodded unconvincingly. Arnold observed her for a moment and then, in an attempt to take her mind off recent events, he said, 'We've just come from the university library. Talking with Miss Hope. Says she knows you.'

Sally nodded. 'I do most of my research there. She's been quite helpful.'

'She asked us to pass on a message. There's someone called at the library recently, asking after you. A man called Dickson. She thought you ought to know, in case it's important.'

Sally stared at him for several seconds, then blinked nervously. She lidded her eyes, a curtain coming down. She shivered slightly, frowned. She seemed on the point of saying something and then thought better of it. She took a deep, shuddering breath. It was as though she had secrets to lose, Arnold thought.

When she said nothing, Portia looked at him meaningfully. 'I think we should take her home,' she suggested. 'And I don't really feel up to going out for a meal now. If you don't mind. We could take Sally back to Wolfcleugh—'

'No,' Sally said, starting out of her reverie. 'I'm not staying there. I mean, it's only the occasional weekend I go up there. I've got digs here in town. I'll be all right. And I wouldn't want to spoil your evening, if you have something planned.'

'I think Portia's right. I'm not in the mood for dinner now either. We've had quite enough excitement for tonight.' He watched her carefully. She was still worried about something: there were shadows of anxiety in her eyes. Perhaps it was because of Semmens. Somehow, Arnold got the impression she had something on her mind. 'We can stay on here with you for a while, if you like, till everything calms down.'

'I'll be all right. It's just . . .' She rubbed her fingers against her forehead. 'It's just that this, coming on top of other things . . . I don't know, I feel as though I'm losing the plot, you know?'

'Are you talking about the Wolfcleugh thing?' Portia asked. 'Because I think we've got some information that might solve things, if we can persuade Steven Burt-Ruckley to support us.'

'Steven?' A vague mist seemed to cloud her eyes and she was lost in thought. Then she shook herself, bringing control back into her mind. 'Families . . . they can be so difficult, can't they? If only people *talked* more, explained things . . .' She hesitated, then frowned as another thought struck her. 'That policeman who came in here. Joe Farley, he said.'

'The name means something?' Arnold asked.

'Nick's girlfriend, up at Wolfcleugh.' Sally looked at him soberly. 'I know she's called Farley.'

There was a short silence. 'You think they are related?'

'I think maybe it was her father,' Sally replied miserably. 'That policeman said he ran a small business. Jenny told me once that her father drove a bulldozer.'

'Ha, it's probably a coincidence,' Portia explained. Sally shook her head. 'I'm not so sure. That man came in here looking for Nick, looking for trouble. And Jenny told me recently that her father was mad at her, for taking up the protest in the woods. You see, as far as I can gather her father was hopeful of getting a contract from the Shangri-La people, to do some of the earth moving in preparation for the road. And he was angry with her, because he saw her support for Nick as taking sides against him, damaging his business.' She frowned, thinking back, and shook her head. 'I think maybe he followed Nick here, came looking for trouble. He's blaming Nick for the hold-up in the work and it's affecting his business.'

'You don't know that,' Arnold said quietly.

'But it makes sense,' she argued sullenly. Then she raised her head as another thought struck her. 'But if he gets mad with Nick about this, what'll he be like when he finds out—' Her voice trailed away.

Portia glanced at Arnold and then turned to the girl. 'Finds out what?'

Sally shook her head mournfully. 'Finds out that Nick has got Jenny Farley pregnant.'

3

Detective Chief Inspector Culpeper was uncomfortable. He felt he had moved beyond matters of general policing years ago. It was simply not his job to deal with matters other than the detection of crime.

The Assistant Chief Constable had not seen it quite like that. 'The fact is, Culpeper, you know how things are at the moment. Half our senior strength are sick with that damned virus and the rest are involved with that trouble up in the north of the county, at Berwick. And then there's the search for that missing teenager — it's drained us and it makes it necessary that we all pull together.'

'But I've already got enough on my plate,' Culpeper protested. 'Can't Farnsby be drafted in to deal with this?'

'He doesn't have the seniority,' the Assistant Chief Constable snapped. 'And anyway, he's away on a course.'

He was always away on bloody courses, Culpeper snarled under his breath. Chief Constable's blue-eyed boy. And the Assistant Chief always kept his nose dean, following the Chief's line and inclinations. He glared at the man across the desk. Assistant Chief Constable Greyson was from down south: an economics graduate who claimed he had entered the police to serve the community. More likely couldn't

get any other bloody job, Culpeper thought sourly, econo-
mists being two a penny. Now he sat there, broad-featured,
large-nosed, bushy-eyebrowed, suggesting Culpeper go back
twenty years and do jobs he'd left far behind him.

But all this was moonshine anyway. The fact was,
Culpeper was on the edge of retirement, he was dispensable,
he could be stuck on any messy job just to get him out of
the way. 'But this is a matter of general policing, sir,' he tried
one last time.

'It's an important matter of general policing,' Greyson
insisted, waving one hand dismissively, 'and one where we
feel violence and disturbance is just around the corner. And
we all know where that can lead.'

Culpeper knew. Broken heads. Bad media coverage.
Claims of police brutality. But he'd left all that behind years
ago. 'Well, if you can assure me, sir, that it's only a matter of
listening and making sympathetic noises—'

'Culpeper, life isn't easy near the top,' the Assistant
Chief confided in a soothing tone. 'I'm subject to all kinds
of pressures. A lot comes down to me to sort. There are
politicians who want things done quickly, their way. There
are businessmen who are convinced that plots are afoot to
damage them. You wouldn't believe the things that cross my
desk.'

Like complaints from friends in the county set, in the
big houses where the Chief Constable was invited to enjoy
himself with the moneyed classes. He'd have passed his wor-
ries on to Greyson. Culpeper knew exactly how it was.

'Anyway, all that you need to do at this stage is hold a
meeting with this man Stafford, get his views, make the usual
assurances and send him on his way happy. A full report to
me afterwards, of course. We don't want to upset this man:
I understand his work, his scheme could be important for
the county.'

'A full report, yes, sir.' Internally, Culpeper groaned. He
lumbered back to his office, overweight, unhappy, resentful
at the way in which life seemed to be whirling him towards

retirement. It was not that he wasn't looking forward to the opportunity to relax, put his feet up, go fishing, spend more time with his wife up at Seahouses. It was just that as the days were counted down he got the impression that he was being side-lined, his wishes and opinions disregarded. That arrogant young bastard Inspector Farnsby was already behaving as if he was going to step into Culpeper's shoes as a matter of form. Not if Culpeper had his way. Farnsby would never make half the copper Culpeper was. Lacked the experience. Didn't know the streets. Hadn't grown up with the villains. Bloody accelerated graduate promotion. Just like the Assistant Chief.

'Good afternoon, gentlemen.' He smiled as he entered the interview room. 'My name is Culpeper. Have you been asked if you would like coffee?'

There were three of them, all dying for coffee. They didn't know the swill that was served up under that name from the canteen. Culpeper smiled and left them briefly to make the arrangements. When he returned, one of the men was standing near the window. He introduced himself. 'I'm Ken Stafford, chief executive of Shangri-La Enterprises. This is my associate Colm Graham. And Mr Smart is in charge of public relations for the company.'

Very smart, Culpeper thought sourly as he shook hands with the sharp-suited, scrubbed-featured young man with the important-looking leather briefcase. He glanced at the others. Stafford himself looked formidable: hard eyes, confident, the assurance that money could bring and something else too — a tough edge. He wouldn't stop at much to gain his ends, Culpeper thought.

And the other man, Colm Graham, now he was something else again. He held Culpeper's glance steadily, but there was something in those eyes Culpeper definitely did not like. Something moved in their depths, like a silent pike seeking its prey. A man who lived on the edge, was Culpeper's guess, a man who had seen violence and could create it. Farnsby wouldn't have seen that, didn't have the experience.

Culpeper was pleased with the thought. It helped him retain the affable smile he displayed to the visitors. 'How can I help you gentlemen?' he asked cheerfully.

Stafford came away from the window and sat down. There was a short pause, then he said, 'It's really by way of an exploratory visit to discuss possible scenarios. You've heard of the Shangri-La developments?'

Culpeper nodded. Bloody expensive fraud, in his view. You could get fresh air and exercise — and a good pint too — at Seahouses, with accommodation a third of the price. But if there were people prepared to pay for . . .

'The fact is we've been held up for several weeks now,' Stafford said, 'but the green light has finally come through from the planning authority. Our access scheme at the edge of Wolfcleugh Woods, we understand it is about to be approved—'

'Congratulations,' Culpeper said hypocritically.

'The thing is, we're expecting trouble.'

'Protester?'

'There are always protesters.' Stafford waved his hand vaguely. 'They're a fact of life in my business. Now, of course, we can hire a security firm, and have one in mind already, to undertake the necessary removal of those who mindlessly bar progress. But in such situations the press often seem to take the side of the great unwashed and we get bad publicity.'

'Which is not what we want at all,' the young man with the scrubbed face intervened somewhat nervously. Stafford glared at him and continued: 'The fact is, we would like to open discussions as to how we can expect . . . collaboration with the police, to avoid any excessive violence up at Wolfcleugh—'

Culpeper was silent for a little while. At last he said, 'I gather they've already built defences in the trees, walkways, all that sort of thing.'

'Unhappily, with the agreement of the landowner,' Stafford remarked stiffly.

'And will you get the permission of the landowner to remove them?'

'That's not exactly my affair. Apparently, legal steps are already being taken. There is a right of way in any case, which the authority has power to improve. In the eventuality, there is a compulsory purchase order in the wings. But that's not the point. What we need to ascertain is what action the police will take, what support they are prepared to give to prevent any unfortunate disturbances at the site.'

'When?' Culpeper asked blandly. His glance slipped away to Colm Graham. The man remained impassive.

'It could be late next week,' Stafford said.

Culpeper grimaced and linked his fingers together, stared at them for a little while. 'It is, of course, always our duty to prevent outbreaks of violence, disturbances, whenever they arise. So I can certainly give you an assurance that we will do all in our power to deal with situations that get out of hand . . . when they get out of hand. At the moment of course, all is peaceful up at Wolfcleugh.'

'Yes, but—'

'The protesters are up in their trees, dreaming their dreams and working on their slogans,' Culpeper said affably. 'The council is still deliberating on giving the approvals you require. Your work force is sitting on its shovels—'

'I take your point,' Stafford interrupted coldly. 'But we feel violence could break out at any moment, and we just want to make sure that the protest doesn't get out of hand. Once it sparks, all sorts of riff-raff will come flocking into the area and unless things are dealt with firmly right at the beginning we could face months of delay. Time none of us can afford.'

'But that's the point, surely,' Culpeper insisted. 'We are not there yet are we? At the beginning, I mean. When we get there, when trouble starts, then we'll be in a position to take action. But I must say,' he added, rising to his feet, 'we're most grateful.'

'For what?' Stafford asked, startled.

'For the public-spirited manner in which you've brought to our attention the likelihood of disturbances up at Wolfcleugh Woods. Now that we have notice of it, when something *does* happen, we'll be able to deal with it decisively. In the meanwhile, I might go up there myself and cast an eye over the place, just to familiarise myself with the problem . . .'

As he saw them off the premises he felt he had handled things very smoothly. Given nothing away. Made no mention of the manpower problems the force was facing. Made no commitment, other than the soothing ones he would have had to make in any case. General policing matters were easy to deal with. And maybe he would take the time to have a look at Wolfcleugh. Long time since he'd had the leisure to go up there, stroll around . . .

As he returned to his office the trolley came along the corridor. On it were four cups of coffee. Best china, he noted. 'Ha, Mavis, what a shame. Too late, I'm afraid. They've gone.'

'But I've brought four cups—' she said indignantly.

'I can manage two,' Culpeper confided. 'And charge them all to the Assistant Chief Constable's account.'

* * *

It wasn't until several days later, on the Friday afternoon, that Culpeper found time to drive up to Wolfcleugh Hill. It was a bright, sunny afternoon, with a cloudless sky and it reminded him of the old days in County Durham, when for a while he had been a beat copper in the west of the county. As he recalled it, there had been less violence in those days, more innocence: young lads would take a warning seriously, local farmers' wives would invite you in for cake and tea, there was less central control on how a man spent his time. As long as he did his rounds, rang in from the beat contact points and dispensed even-handed, rough justice, the occasional clip on the ear when it was called for, no one seemed to mind very much. Things were different now.

But then, they'd become different as soon as he left the uniformed branch. And over the years it had all been a slow, steady deterioration. He grunted. Did all old men feel that way?

He parked at the edge of the woods and looked about him. The hill sloped down gently away to his left, across the expanse of low-lying bogland that was Wolfcleugh Moss. Just below him he could see a wooden shack, exposed earth and peat, and some people crouching in a trench. The archaeologists, he concluded. He was more concerned with the present than the past. And, he supposed, the future, as far as these woods were concerned.

He strolled along the narrow path into the woods. The late afternoon sun slanted through the trees, dappling the path, and it was all very quiet and very peaceful. Bracken crunched under his feet, the soil was peaty and brown, and a fluttering in the trees above his head suggested pigeons nesting there. A magpie flashed above his head, black and white. Shortly afterwards he thought he caught the sound of voices and to his left, along the verge of the road glimpsed through the trees, he saw some elderly vehicles parked. Then the trees thinned and he came into the edge of a clearing.

He looked about him. The ground was trampled here, there was the sound of sawing some distance off and a fire smoked at the far edge of the clearing. The protesters were gathering, he realised. He counted maybe fifteen people moving around in a fairly purposeful fashion, stopping to chat, some carrying sawn-off timbers that looked suspiciously like stakes and clubs, and above his head he noted the swaying ropes and walkways. A couple of men stopped and stared at him but he ignored them: if they had a right to be here, so had he. It was a public right of way, after all.

One of the men walked forward, ponytailed, arrogant. 'Who are you?'

Culpeper ignored him for a moment, continuing his inspection, then he looked at him and smiled. 'I'm the fuzz.'

'We're doing nothing wrong,' the man said, startled.

'Only damaging the environment.'

'We're here to save it!'

'So I'm told.' Culpeper brushed past him, strolled forward into the clearing. 'Getting ready for a siege, then, hey?'

'We're not looking for trouble,' the man replied sullenly.

Culpeper noted the bruises on his face, the swollen lip. 'Seems like you've had some already. And now you're preparing for more, yeah?' Culpeper watched the men wandering around the clearing. They looked young, scruffy — a mixture of weedy, earnest endeavour mingled with shaven-headed muscle.

'So what do you want here?'

'Just out for an afternoon stroll, bonny lad, nothing more. Taking the air and having a look at what you people are up to. What's your name, son?'

'Semmens.'

'All right. Well, enjoy your little working holidays up here and don't cause too much damage. I hope we don't have to meet again. But then, the world's an uncertain place, isn't that right?'

Culpeper turned and retraced his steps, whistling lightly. Not many people whistled these days, he considered, when he was a young man everyone seemed to whistle. He wondered why that was.

So the weekend brigade were arriving to build up numbers at Wolfcleugh. That's maybe what it was: a sort of working weekend in the open air, a getting away from the job to help a cause. Or maybe there was something more to it. Perhaps the word was out, maybe a whisper was in the air that a decision was expected soon and it was time for the forces of resistance to gather.

He shook his head. Maybe the boys would soon all be on overtime again, fighting other people's battles . . .

* * *

Wolfcleugh Woods were quiet at night. On summer evenings, when the sky above hardly seemed to darken at all, retaining a deep blue scattered with bright stars, the depths of the woods were silent except for the occasional scuffling of small mammals and the brushing wings of hunting owls.

For the men and women who were sleeping there, cocooned in their sleeping bags in small tents, there was no feeling of fear. They heard the occasional snuffling, shifting sounds of sexual activity from some of the tents, the grunting of disturbed sleep, and smelled the drifting woodsmoke that still emerged from the damped-down fires. Many of them were townspeople, campers perhaps, but not well used to the country air and the silence of the woods.

And they were too young, too inexperienced to be aware of the history of Wolfcleugh, of the death and violence it had seen over the millennia. They would know nothing of the chanting of shamans, the drifting incantations that called to the bear and the wolf and the eagle, the quick knife at the throat, the broken back, the living interments in the peaty soil. Perhaps folk memory stirred in their dreams briefly. Perhaps the snuffling they imagined they heard was only in their ancient minds, that part of the dream state that they had inherited from long-dead ancestors clad in wolf pelts.

But they began to struggle from their deep sleep when they saw the lights and heard the stuttering roar of engines. The threatening, wary peace of the woods was shattered and they staggered drunkenly from their slumbers. There was a confused shouting, lights slashed through the air and the trees were lit up garishly, nakedly, as the roaring sound increased.

Panic ensued, as they came. There were two of them, advancing into the woods, smashing aside the undergrowth, crushing and growling and tearing their way forward. Young alder were uprooted, oaks were scarred by the broad, vicious blades, birch screamed and bent, and gave way under the onslaught.

The protesters were running aimlessly, panicked, inco- herent. Some scrambled up the rope ladders to the presumed safety of the trees, some huddled at the edge of the clearing, young women clutching blankets around their shoulders, wide-eyed, frightened. A small group gathered around the ponytailed man, waving his arms, shouting unintelligible orders against the din, the roar of the bulldozers, and men began picking up clubs, making frantic gestures, yelling incoherently, milling around like frustrated bulls, helpless without a plan of defence, hopeless in the face of the menacing, roaring steel that faced them and advanced on them inexorably.

The machines had come in from the roadway, torn through the fence that defended the woods and were cutting a great swathe along the narrow track that formed the public right of way. They crashed forward into the clearing, swung again, attacked the trees and walkways tumbled, crashing down as the trees shuddered under the onslaught. Then they swung again, one machine leading the other, a dark man at the controls roaring above the sound of his own engines, gesticulating furiously, a hand punching the night sky. The protesters scattered like rabbits before the attack, then gathered at the edge of the clearing, screaming abuse, throwing stones, dancing with rage, until at last the bulldozers turned, the lights glared across white faces, teeth grinning with hate and fury, and they went back along the great raw swathe they had created into the clearing camp.

The noise continued long after the roaring had faded and the bulldozers had made their way back down the hill. Some of the women were crying; two people nursed slight injuries, scratches, sprains; one small group of angry men was being harangued by the wild-eyed, spitting, ponytailed man who screamed of the revenge of the underclass, and the coming of revolution and violence.

Gradually the fury died and miserable resentment nursed its grievances in a low muttering of complaint, interspersed with vows. The night was half over and there were hints of dawn streaking the early sky, stars fading in the dark blue, gold rising in the east, high above the trees. Sleep was impossible and unsought; the camp was a shambles. Crushed tents, torn undergrowth, scarred trees, collapsed walkways — there was too much to do by way of repair, too much talking and crying to do, too much anger and resentment, and threats to make.

One of the young women pulled her resentment into decision and rebuilt the fire. A coffee pot was produced; the smell of coffee soon mingled with the tang of the woodsmoke. They gathered around the fire, arguing, still furious, but misery also intruded. The coffee helped alleviate it, as they talked and planned, and vowed they would never be moved.

One long-haired young man in scruffy jeans and polo-necked sweater moved off to relieve himself in the broken bushes, down near the edge of the woods, where the great scar caused by the bulldozers was deep and rutted. He had been drinking heavily before he had fallen asleep. The excitement had extended his bladder to bursting point. He was still a little unsteady on his feet when he splashed away in the rutted track.

He came back, hoping to lighten the atmosphere. He held something long and dark in his hand.

'Hey,' he called out, giggling drunkenly. 'Anyone lost a bone?'

CHAPTER THREE

1

Arnold was appalled when he saw the carnage.

Portia had come into his office on the Monday morning. 'Did you see the local news this morning?'

Arnold had not, but the gossip had already been running through the department. 'I gather it's started.'

'Trouble? You can say that again.' Portia shook her head. 'What the hell could have got into those idiots? The decision hasn't been announced by the council. There was no need for this sort of violence. Now it's got everyone's back up. Anyway, Karen wants us in her office. Like *now!*'

It was as though she regarded the whole situation as their fault alone, Arnold thought as he looked at Karen Stannard. She was in a towering rage. Oddly enough, Arnold felt that he had never seen her looking more beautiful. Her colour was heightened, emphasising her tan. Her magnificent eyes seemed to spark with fury, her breasts strained against the formal white blouse and she strode around the office like a frustrated leopard. 'This throws everything into the melting pot!' she exclaimed. 'It places everyone in an impossible position! I can't imagine what's got into these people. Is Ken Stafford crazy? The council was on the point of issuing a statement and the idiot takes the law into his own hands and attacks the protest site! You can imagine what's going to happen now — they'll bloody well flock to the scene! All the riff-raff, the New Age travellers, the shaven-headed New Front, every hooligan within a hundred miles who likes a good fight with broken bottles on a Saturday night. Can you *imagine!*'

Arnold had already envisaged the consequences. Portia, too, was enraged. As they had walked down the corridor towards Karen Stannard's office, she had complained that this turn in events could also destroy whatever hope she might have had of getting her report accepted.

Now the thought was emphasised to her by Karen Stannard herself. 'And this,' the Acting Director of the department said in a cool, vicious tone, 'makes your own efforts a complete waste of time, doesn't it? I read your report — your *dissenting* report over the weekend. A pity: you make out quite an interesting case for the Reverend Hatch and his discoveries to be treated seriously and I was almost persuaded that you should be allowed to present it to the council. Not that they would have taken any notice of it of course, sentiment of that kind would never sway them. You see, Portia, you've underestimated the situation. I've been right all along. You both thought I was bending to the pressure of politicians and businessmen but I wasn't, I was merely being realistic. An extension of the bog excavations into the woods was never a realistic possibility, no matter how many Hatches you dug up! There's always been too much riding on this — too much money, too many reputations.'

She marched around the room, folding and unfolding her arms. 'Now we're likely to find ourselves right in the middle of a real mess. We'll be asked for views again. We'll be made scapegoats. They'll say it's due to the delays in our department that all this has come to a head now. If the council had announced its decision earlier. If action had been taken before now . . . it's we who'll be blamed, dammit!'

It was Karen herself who had caused the delay, Arnold thought, but didn't say. 'I think you're over-reacting,' he said quietly. 'No one is going to lay this at our door.'

She stopped, stared at him angrily and for a moment he thought she was going to lose her temper completely. Then reason reasserted itself and she calmed down, took her seat behind her desk, steepled her fingers, touching her mouth as she regarded Arnold and Portia carefully. She nodded. 'All right, Arnold, maybe you're right. So tell me. What do we do now?'

He shrugged. 'It's not strictly a departmental problem. The protesters have been attacked, but nothing else has changed. Your report has gone in—'

'While mine has been shelved, of course,' Portia spat.

Karen Stannard ignored her.

Arnold went on, 'I understand the opposition to the whole plan will now grow: there are already reports of militant groups gathering to join Semmens and his protesters. Almost inevitably, if it escalates, the police will be drawn in, if they haven't been already . . .'

'Yes, I know,' Karen interrupted him irritably, 'but Powell Frinton will be asking me, what we do now.'

'I don't see that it's our problem,' Arnold insisted. 'You say the authority has already accepted your report before they've seen Portia's. They've made the decision, though it hasn't been announced. Sensibly, they should stay low for a while, keep their heads down. So should we.'

'I'm not so certain. The issues are still there. Shangri-La want to build their road. The council is supporting them. Diane Power wants a halt to it so she can extend her researches into the wood line. The protesters want to stop the road completely. The owner, Burt-Ruckley is sitting on the bloody fence: he doesn't want this and he won't support that. He's only interested in keeping his bloody woodland sacrosanct. I just have this gut feeling that at some stage everyone is going to point a finger and it's going to be at us!' She shook her head, sighing in angry frustration. 'I don't know . . . Portia, I want another copy of your report for the file. I'll go over it again. Maybe there is something in it we can use, if the council starts looking for a way out of the decision they've already taken. My holding it back might have been the right way after all.'

Portia opened her mouth to protest at the assumption, but Arnold shot her a warning glance. Better to have the report accepted this way than not at all. Karen Stannard looked at Arnold. 'Meanwhile, let me get on with working out the strategy. You, Arnold, you'd better get up to the site and take a look at the whole situation. Have a word with Diane Power. See if she's been affected. And you, Portia . . .' She fixed her with a sharp, green-eyed glance. 'You might as well go with him. The pair of you seem to be thick as thieves these days, anyway.'

* * *

And the situation had been worse than Arnold had imagined. Even from the archaeological dig site he could see how savaged the edge of Wolfcleugh Woods had been. The track itself had been torn up, the fence and wiring destroyed, perhaps fifteen trees felled, a wide swathe driven through across the public right of way, raw earth exposed, deep ruts running into the clearing, trees scarred, leaning crazily.

And among it all, like scurrying ants, a small army of young people, building, erecting, constructing, sawing, hammering. The protest army had arrived.

'It's as though they're building a fortress up there,' Dr Power said.

Arnold nodded and glanced at her. She looked weary, somehow. Perhaps she had been affected by the sight of the damage, by the thought that so much could have been destroyed up there in the area she had been hoping to excavate. 'There have been no problems down here?' he asked.

She shook her head. 'No. I was here on site early on Sunday morning, when I heard there'd been trouble. It's all happened up there, on the other side of the road. I think some scavenging has gone on down here, probably people belonging to Semmens: a few planks of wood, some drainpipes we were intending to use, but nothing serious. The bulldozers concentrated their activity up there. We've not really been affected. But, I don't know . . . I was hoping that we could make out a case for the extension of work up there. Now, it's all going to be submerged under the wave of recriminations over this shambles.' She grunted to herself. *'People . . .'*

Arnold knew how she felt. 'Well, since you haven't really been hit by any problems, we'll leave you to it. You'll have a lot of distant disturbance I guess, from now on, but if you can handle that . . .'

'If any of that mob come down here,' she said menacingly, 'they'll get more than they bargained for.' Arnold looked again at her muscular frame and thought she was probably right. He nodded to Portia. 'Come on, let's go take a look up there.'

They climbed the hill slowly, crossing the swathe of broken ground, and entered Wolfcleugh Woods. The activity seemed well organised. There was no sign of Nick Semmens but Arnold caught a glimpse of Jenny Farley, shirt-sleeved, high in one of the trees, repairing a walkway. As Dr Power had suggested, they were building a fortress. Some of them were singing, he noted, and there was a general air of purpose about it all.

Portia wandered off, looking about her in a distracted manner. Arnold caught sight of a solitary policeman, standing near the edge of the clearing, looking somewhat bored. Arnold walked across to him and nodded. 'A mess.'

'You could say that, sir.'

'Anyone injured?'

'Nothing serious.' The constable looked at him and frowned. 'And you would be, sir—?'

'My name's Landon. Department of Museums and Antiquities. We'd been doing a report on the area concerning the Shangri-La roadway.'

'I see.' The young, fresh-faced policeman looked about him. 'There's going to be trouble over that now, right enough.'

Arnold nodded and walked away. He hesitated briefly, wondering whether he should go to talk to some of the people repairing the tree walkways and then thought better of it.

Portia was walking slowly along the rutted ground as though looking for something. As he made his way down to her she suddenly stopped, raised her head. 'Arnold!'

There was an urgency in her tone that startled him.

He quickened his pace. She stood there, rigid, staring down at her feet. When he reached her, she pointed down wordlessly.

The scarred earth that had been torn up by the bulldozers on Saturday night had left a deep rutted track. The soil itself was dry and friable, though peaty, thick with twisted tree and scrub roots. But where the material had been thrown back by the harsh ripping blade of the bulldozer Arnold could see something protruding from the earth. He knelt down, put out a hand.

It was several seconds before he realised what he was touching. It was the well-preserved remains of a right foot, with the ragged skin of the lower leg attached.

* * *

Detective Chief Inspector Culpeper scratched his head and yawned. He'd had a bad night. He and his wife had been married for over thirty years now and she would still from time to time give him a massive fry-up which, though he devoured it without a thought, would give him massive heartburn during the night. He shook his head. You'd have thought the woman would have had more sense, after all these years.

Like he should have had more sense, believing the business up at Wolfcleugh would be nothing more than a quiet bit of general police work, which he could handle without undue effort. But no sooner had he agreed to help out than things were beginning to unravel. The affray up at the woods on Saturday night had got people up in arms, and the Assistant Chief Constable had already made it clear to Culpeper that he thought it was his fault. Quite what was the logic behind that view escaped Culpeper, but he didn't argue with Greyson, not when he was in that sort of cold rage.

At least they had the ringleader in custody.

He made his way down the stairs at headquarters in Ponteland and walked along to the interview room, where they had brought in the miscreant for questioning. He'd spent one night in the cells, and it wasn't the first, Culpeper noted with interest as he inspected the sheet in his hands. His lips framed the name: 'Joseph Farley.'

There were two coppers in the room with Farley — a recently promoted sergeant and a woman police officer. The three of them were sitting there with cups of coffee, proper little party, Culpeper thought savagely. At least only Farley was smoking. He nodded to the sergeant, then jerked his head. The officer got quickly to his feet, hesitated, picked up his coffee cup and left. Culpeper glared balefully at the WPC and she also rose, backed against the wall and stood there, stony-faced.

Culpeper sat down in front of Farley and stared at him: tough, belligerent face, marked with sullenness, short-cropped hair, greying; muscular frame; open-necked check shirt; dirty jeans; a faint smell of oil. Culpeper shook his head in mock dismay. 'Fun and games, hey, Joe? Fun and games.'

Farley made no reply.

'You been having a right time of it just recently, haven't you? Makes a man like me despair. I mean, a run-in with the law down on Tyneside, smashing up a pub in the city, drunk and disorderly conduct—'

'I wasn't drunk,' Farley interjected in a surly tone.

'Oh, so that makes it all right, to take a pub apart if you're not drunk? What was all that about, anyway, if it wasn't a drunken brawl?'

Farley shrugged. 'Private matter.'

'Most fist fights are, I suppose. You got a night in the cells to cool off . . . but it didn't seem to make any differ-ence. Let me see . . . yes, here we are.' Culpeper peered at the notes in his file. 'Saturday night, you and a mate — works for you, it seems, Charlie Edwards, no form you pair get it in your heads to go rousting out those poor young innocents up at Wolfcleugh Wood and you really make a go of it, don't you! Trouble is, you can't really do a runner when you're trundling a bulldozer along country lanes in the middle of the night, can you? And there's such a thing as mobile phones these days. So what happens, one of those poor young things—'

'Bloody parasites. Half of them never done a day's work in their lives!'

'—one of them,' Culpeper continued, 'a young lady, in quite a state it seems, she rings up the boys in blue and there we are, on the scene in minutes—'

'More like an hour, more like,' Farley jeered. 'Another ten minutes and we'd have been off the road and away.'

'Like the Great Train Robbers, hey? Spirited away into the distance. No matter, Joe, it didn't happen like that, did it. Patrol car spotted you, creeping along through the hedgerows, no lights, but making a hell of a racket on a quiet night. Catch you for speeding, did he?'

Farley was contemptuous of Culpeper's heavy sarcasm. He made no answer, but stared into his empty coffee cup. 'Any chance of more coffee?'

'Coffee, my arse,' Culpeper replied amicably. 'You better get serious. We've got you for criminal damage, at least, my lad. But maybe you can give us good reason why you were bouncing around up there at Wolfcleugh. Maybe you can persuade us it was all in a good cause. You know what the magistrates are like, where good causes are concerned.'

Farley squinted at him thoughtfully. 'They was trespassin' up there.'

'No. Won't wash. They had permission to nest in those trees like sweet little pigeons. Try again.'

'It was personal.'

Culpeper leaned back in his chair and stretched. 'Now, I don't quite see it like that. Funny thing, you know, only a couple of days ago I had some fellas in here. One of them name of Stafford. He was sort of telling me that there'd be trouble up there at Wolfcleugh, because his legitimate business aspirations was being foiled by irresponsible tearaways all set on impeding his progress, destroying his plans to build a roadway up there. And then, not so long afterwards, lo and behold, as they used to say in all the best dramatic texts, you go up there with a couple of bulldozers and try to solve a problem for him. Is that the way it was, Farley? Were you doing a sort of favour for Mr Stafford?'

Farley displayed a degree of agitation. 'It wasn't like that. It was nothing to do with Mr Stafford.'

'Oh, come on, Joe! You're not going to tell me it was all a bit of Saturday night fun!'

Farley twisted in his seat uncomfortably and glanced at the woman police officer. 'It was just . . . personal.'

'How?'

'It was that bastard Nick Semmens I was after.'

'Semmens?' Culpeper frowned and consulted his notes. 'It was Semmens you were involved with in that Newcastle pub. The Northumberland Arms.'

'Ponytailed bastard.'

Of course, Culpeper thought. The bruised young man he himself had had a chat with, up Wolfcleugh. 'So what have you got against Semmens?'

Joe Farley was silent for a little while. And then it all came rushing out of him on a tide of resentment. 'I worked hard all my life, you know that? All right, there was a time when I was a bit of a tearaway, but what youngster in the trade doesn't get the occasional wild Saturday night? But I grew away from all that. I got responsibilities: a wife, a daughter. I got my act together, I started out sensibly again, after that time I spent in the nick—'

'Three years.' Culpeper nodded, consulting his file. 'Bad mistake, going to burgle with a pick handle. You were lucky you didn't break the householder's back.'

'That was before. I changed after that,' Farley insisted. 'One stretch was enough for me. And I started this small business, you know? Began to build it up. And last year I got hold of three' dozers. On hire, OK, but in a couple of years they'd be mine, you know? And I got the sniff of a contract with Ken Stafford's company. I laid out the money, see? I was counting on the work starting this month. And then that bastard Semmens started shouting his mouth off. Never done a day's work in his life, but screams about the environment, sits up there in the trees like a bloody monkey and causes the sort of trouble, the delays that mean my contract with Stafford is held up and I'm paying out good money, and the bank's on my back—'

'And you thought you'd move things along a bit by taking the law into your own hands and knocking them out of their trees?' Culpeper shook his head in wonder. 'You can't really believe that would have solved the problem.'

Farley shrugged sullenly.

Culpeper was silent for a while. He sniffed doubtfully. 'So it was just frustration that sent you up there, frustration at the delay, because you could see a contract slipping away and you wanted to try to shake them out of the trees. That's it?'

Farley made no reply.

'And you acted on your own initiative? No one put you up to it? Stafford wasn't involved?'

'Nothin' to do with Mr Stafford.'

'So why wasn't your frustration overcome when you caught Semmens, earlier, in the Northumberland Arms? Why did you try to beat the hell out of him and then still go up to Wolfcleugh to have another go?'

'I told you. It was personal.'

'It must have been. You keep telling me so. But what was personal about it?' Culpeper pressed.

There was a short silence. Furtively, Joe Farley glanced at the woman police officer and then glared at Culpeper with fierce eyes. 'I got a daughter. I brought her up proper—'

'When you weren't inside.'

Farley didn't like that. His nostrils flared angrily. 'She's sixteen now and she's got a mind of her own. But she's been led astray. That bastard Semmens — he persuaded her to join him in that bloody stupid protest and nothin' I could do to stop it. I was in town, I saw him go into that pub, I parked my van and I went in there after him. He had this bird with him, some little whore from the Wolfcleugh camp, and he was sittin' there, chattin' her up and I was all set to lay into him, and I would have seen him to rights too, if the polis hadn't arrived—'

'You went after him because he was buying some woman a drink in the pub?' Culpeper asked wanderingly.

'He's been screwin' my daughter!' Farley blazed. 'And there he was, tryin' it on with some other slut while Jenny was waiting for him up at Wolfcleugh guarding their precious camp!'

There was a light tap on the door. Culpeper glanced back, to see the sergeant opening it. 'Can I have a word, sir?'

Culpeper stepped outside and bent his head as the sergeant murmured in his ear. Culpeper straightened, frowned and felt a slight surge of satisfaction. He nodded, turned and went back into the room. He sat down in front of Farley, joviality itself. 'Funny thing,' he confided. 'I wasn't very happy dealing with all this business. Not exactly my scene, you see, Joe — left this kind of thing years ago. Spent too long out of uniform to want to go back. So, what do we have here? Assault and battery on this Semmens character. Malicious damage up at Wolfcleugh, maybe attempted GBH. Not bad. Enough to go on. But now, something else's turned up.' He grinned at Farley, a malicious glint in his eyes. 'You know, Joe, you should know better. Runnin' around in the dark with a bloody big tractor. All sorts of accidents can happen. Particularly with panicked youngsters scattering, screaming, half asleep, not knowing where to run, with the lights and the noise and the crashing trees. Must have been quite a scene. Like out of hell.'

Joe Farley straightened in his chair. 'What are you rabbitin' on about?'

'What I'm rabbitin' on about is this, Joe Farley. I don't think we're just talking about malicious damage and personal vendettas any longer. It's dangerous, drivin' about in the dark on a bulldozer, like I said. And we've just had a call from the copper on site up at Wolfcleugh. Seems like in the tracks of your bloody machine they've found what looks like a woman's foot. And no one up there is claiming it at the moment. So unless someone does, looks like there's the chance she *can't* claim it, because maybe she got run down in the dark. Now at the very least, Joe, that's manslaughter.' He showed his teeth, grimacing satisfaction. 'And at the worst, it could be murder!'

2

Steven Burt-Ruckley was clearly disturbed. He seemed greyer
somehow. His eyes were dark-shadowed and there was a blu-
ish line of strain around his mouth. He sat unbending but
clearly nervous in the chair in Powell Frinton's office, a disregarded cold cup of coffee on the low desk in front of him,
Karen Stannard, grim-featured, to his left. When Arnold
entered he could see from Powell Frinton's attitude that the
discussion had not been going well.

'Mr Landon. Please come in and sit down.' The chief
executive pointed a bony finger at the empty chair beside
Karen Stannard. 'We thought it might be useful if you were
to join this discussion, since you are the person responsible
for the oversight of the Wolfcleugh Woods situation.'

Arnold shot a sharp glance at Karen Stannard: this was
the first time he knew he was in charge. She stared straight
ahead, avoiding his eyes.

'I have had certain representations from the council members,' Powell Frinton continued in a tone that emphasised his
displeasure, 'and this morning Mr Burt-Ruckley has been kind
enough to come in to talk things over with us. Perhaps, sir . . . ?'

Burt-Ruckley's mouth twisted slightly, as though he had
difficulty getting the words out. 'The situation has become

intolerable,' he announced harshly. 'My property rights are being invaded, my wishes ignored, the handling of the whole business has become a shambles and the time has come to put an end to all this passing the buck.'

They all looked at Arnold. Startled, he said, 'I haven't been up to Wolfcleugh for a few days. I hadn't realised—'

'Then perhaps I had better explain the present situation,' Burt-Ruckley interrupted. 'I understand it was you who made the discovery of those remains after the bulldozer attack in the woods.'

'Well, yes, Miss Tyrrel and I . . . though I should add that there were in fact two discoveries. Immediately after the attack in the darkness one of the students apparently found a thigh bone. He did not produce it until after we came across the remains in the ground. The police had asked us to stay there after we found the foot, until someone came out from Morpeth to take our statements. That's when the young student came wandering down, to find out what was happening, and produced his own find. The interesting thing about the bone was—'

'I'm not interested in bones,' Burt-Ruckley snapped.

His eyes were restless, almost panicky. 'I'm concerned about what's happening on my land. Do you know that it's like a circus up there?'

'As I said, I've not been up—'

'A brawling circus.' Burt-Ruckley seemed to be having difficulty keeping his temper. His skin was mottled with suppressed anger and his hand was shaking slightly. 'I am not a reclusive man, in my view, I keep to myself and always have done over the years. I lead a quiet life and pursue those interests that attract me. I make charitable donations. But I'm not a joiner. I don't like people trampling over my lands. I love the peace and quiet of Wolfcleugh. I wanted it all left as it has been for a thousand years. But that's now all changed. I've been to those people I know on the council, but they merely direct me to talk to officials. Like yourselves. So I want to know what you're doing about it.'

Helplessly Arnold looked at Powell Frinton. The chief executive's features were unreadable, his cold eyes were fixed on Arnold. 'It seems that the police have cordoned off the area where the . . . remains were discovered. They're treating the matter as a murder enquiry, for the moment.'

Arnold raised his eyebrows. 'I know they'll have to go through the form there, but in my view—'

'I'm not interested in your *views*,' Burt-Ruckley rasped. 'I demand action. The police . . . I understand that we can do nothing about that. They have their duties to perform. I'm not quibbling about that. But the unfortunate thing is that the newspapers have got their teeth into the story, no doubt from someone in this office—'

'I assure you,' Arnold began warmly, 'that no one to my knowledge—'

'Protestations are easy,' Burt-Ruckley sneered. 'The fact is the media are making a big play out of all this. Consequently, a considerable number of people have taken to hanging around at the fringe of the police operations. Not just reporters, but what I would describe as ghouls, idiots who want a vicarious thrill, excited merely at being at the scene. There are some who are camping there. And now a degree of friction has begun to arise between them and the protesters. There have been arguments, largely about the use of the area. It is littered with cans, rubbish . . . *this is my land, you understand!*' There was an edge of hysteria in his tone.

Arnold stared at him. He gained the impression Burt-Ruckley was close to breaking point. 'I'm sorry,' he replied gently. 'But I don't see what we can do. It's a matter for the police and for you—'

Karen Stannard cut in suddenly. Her glance, directed at Arnold, was frosty. 'I think it's only fair to say that we've all been somewhat too *focused* in our views of what should be done. Quite rightly, Mr Burt-Ruckley has been trying to preserve the integrity of his boundaries. He has not wanted the Shangri-La development and took the steps he thought necessary to try to prevent it, other than by going to the courts. On reflection, perhaps that was a mistake. Giving the protesters permission to camp up there was, with hindsight, an unwise step to take.'

Burt-Ruckley said nothing, but his lips tightened and he stared straight ahead of him. He was probably of the same opinion, but unwilling to admit it.

'I cannot speak for the politicians, of course,' she went on, 'but from my earlier discussions with Mr Powell Frinton, it seems they are now a little concerned at the possible effects of their decision — which has yet to be publicly released — and are seeking some compromise way out of the dilemma. They fear that if things go on as they are, disorder might spread and the police will have to take action. On the other hand, there is still a powerful lobby within the council which argues they should not be frightened off a decision merely by the newspapers and the mob in the trees.'

Arnold could guess at the scenario: half the council members scared at the thought of bad publicity and disturbances, the other half being pressured by Ken Stafford and fearful that the reasons for their support of the scheme might become public know ledge. They wouldn't have been acting in support of Stafford for nothing. Stafford would have bought their loyalty.

Karen Stannard glanced around her, fixing their attention. 'It seems to me that we all have to reach some kind of compromise. Much will depend on the police report, of course, but let me explain that while I had prepared and submitted a report of my own to the council, to support the Shangri-La development, I have always held back, for good reasons which have now been exonerated, a second view of the whole situation.'

Powell Frinton raised his head slightly, like a pointer sniffing the wind.

'We need to look at how we can get out of the dilemma we find ourselves facing. Mr Burt-Ruckley wants to preserve privacy on his land. We in the department want to preserve what we regard as our environment and our heritage. Shangri-La

Enterprises want their road. The council want to be let off the hook. Perhaps, if everyone is prepared to compromise . . .'

'In what way?' Burt-Ruckley asked harshly, suspicion staining his eyes.

'First of all, I have asked for a report to be prepared about the extent of Wolfcleugh Moss two hundred years ago.'

Arnold stared at her. This was vintage Karen. She had thrown aside with contempt the report Portia had given her. Now she was claiming credit for commissioning it.

'The study shows that Wolfcleugh Woods have steadily encroached upon the Moss, through drainage, agriculture, climatic change over the years. The wooded area is larger than it used to be. And there is evidence to show that in the past bodies have, been found within the area that is now covered by the woodland. In other words, it is highly likely that there is more to be found by way of archaeological investigation, within the woods, where the old margins of the Moss were formerly located.'

Burt-Ruckley's breathing was irregular. 'What are you trying to say?'

'I am suggesting that we release the report to the council, persuade them to reverse their decision on the grounds that the woods should be declared a heritage site.'

'So that Shangri-La would not be allowed to drive through with their road?'

Karen Stannard nodded.

Burt-Ruckley ran a tongue over dry lips. 'A heritage site . . . what would that mean in practice?'

'We would have to show the public that we're serious about it. We'd have to show Ken Stafford that he'd be fighting a lost cause. It means, sir, you would have to give permission for Dr Diane Power and her team to extend their investigations into the old bog margins now in the wooded area.'

'I'm not happy with that.'

'I understand, sir, but I stress again, some compromise is necessary,' Karen urged softly.

'Exactly how would they do that — extend their investigations?' Burt-Ruckley asked doubtfully.

'Probably by running an exploratory trench, much along the lines of the present investigation,' Karen explained. 'Not immediately, of course, since they're fully occupied with their present work. But plans could be drawn up . . . the actual work probably would not start for a year or two. But a start would have to be made, to convince everyone we're serious . . .'

Arnold watched Burt-Ruckley with interest. Something was flickering in his eyes, dampened fires, uneasiness, concern. He swallowed nervously. The words seemed to be dragged out reluctantly. 'That sounds a possibility. But Shangri-La would never go along with the suggestion. And with the political pressure they can mount—'

'They would have to be offered an alternative route,' Powell Frinton said bluntly. 'I have already discussed this with the planning department and Miss Stannard. There is another possible route. The access road could run to the west of your woods at Wolfcleugh, Mr Burt-Ruckley. It would be more expensive, of course, because the detour would involve a longer, looping access route. Shangri-La would face increased expenditure. But a lot of trouble would be avoided.'

'West of Wolfcleugh Hill,' Burt-Ruckley said reluctantly. 'It would mean I would have to give up some of my land there. It seems to me I am the one losing here. I am the one making all the compromises. I give up some land west of Wolfcleugh Hill and I allow entrenchment into my woods for archaeological activity. The next thing you'll be doing is asking me to provide funds to cover Shangri-La's extra expenditure!'

There was something feeble about the protest. Arnold caught the gleam in Karen's eye as she too recognised that Burt-Ruckley was weakening, not entirely against the proposal. 'I did suggest that *everyone* had to compromise. That includes Shangri-La Enterprises.'

There was a long silence, as Burt-Ruckley sat deep in thought. At last he sniffed and rose to his feet. 'I shall give your proposal due consideration.'

There was a triumphant edge to Karen Stannard's smile. She knew that Burt-Ruckley was prepared to accept the compromise.

* * *

The following morning an impassive Ken Stafford sat in Powell Frinton's office and listened to the proposal. Arnold was present, but on this occasion Karen Stannard had seen fit to absent herself, pleading other work, a pre-arranged meeting at Amble. She had every confidence, she had explaining winningly to Arnold, that the matter could be left safely in his hands.

The man from the Planning Department was Fred Curry, an old acquaintance of Arnold's. He had himself worked in that department originally, before clashes with the then departmental head had led to his reassignment to Museums and Antiquities.

Curry had brought a rolled-up plan of the Wolfcleugh area and, at Powell Frinton's invitation, he spread it out for inspection. 'Here's the Moss and the woods. Here's the original line of the proposed access road to the valley, cutting along here. Now, the new suggestion runs like this. From the main junction here' — he stabbed a stubby finger on the map — 'the access road would be routed around to the west. It would cut through this farm here, but that's no problem because old Arthur has been wanting to get rid of that stretch of field for years, sour land, he says, so Shangri-La could get it for a song. The road would then climb along the ridge here. Great views from up there, right across the valley. People coming to Shangri-La would have a grand prospect spread out before them . . . Anyway, from there it would run here, crossing this stream, well, it's just a beck really and would raise no engineering problems, and then dip down into the valley and your planned site.' He leaned back, pleased with himself. 'Seems to me it would solve all your problems.'

Ken Stafford inspected the map carefully, tracing the line with his finger, checking the varying heights of the land as delineated by the contour lines. He took several minutes over the task, frowning hard. 'Solve all *your* problems, maybe. Not mine.' He looked up, glared at Powell Frinton. 'It's not acceptable.'

'My dear sir . . . may I ask why?' Powell Frinton enquired in a reedy tone, edged with frustration.

'Finance. Simple as that. All my estimates, all my costs are based on the line of the access road proposed for planning permission. This road starts off a whole new ball game. Just look at it: we'd be running west for perhaps an extra three miles. We'd be crossing rising land and then dipping down again. We have farmland to acquire — at whatever cost — a stream to deal with. Now, you talk of compromise, but I ask who's going to cover all the extra cost of this proposal?' He raised a cynical eyebrow at Powell Frinton. 'Here I am, bringing an amenity to the valley below Wolfcleugh. I'm bringing in work. I'm bringing in jobs. Everyone agrees the development of a Shangri-La Country Park is just what the valley needs to regenerate it economically. And now you want me to throw all my access plans on to the dust heap and start again. Fine. But will the council stump up the extra money?'

Powell Frinton coughed as though something was sticking in his throat. 'We all know, Mr Stafford, that this is a purely commercial development—'

'Exactly. In other words, the county won't stump up. That means my company will have to pay. Commercial decision, you say? Exactly. My decision. And the decision is definitely negative. No. This solution, as you call it, is not acceptable.'

'But Mr Burt-Ruckley and the council—'

Ken Stafford's face was suddenly suffused with anger. 'Let me tell you about bloody Burt-Ruckley and the council. To start with, we have a man who can't seem to make up his mind what he wants. He's been fence-sitting, hoping the problem will go away. He raised the stakes in all this by allowing those damned yobs to camp on his land, with the explicit purpose and intention of slowing down this whole development, putting pressure on the council. The man needs locking up. He's living in the past; he's a waste of time.' Stafford jabbed a finger in Powell Frinton's direction. 'And then there's the council. They're like a bunch of scared sheep. I put a proposal to them, they consult their lawyers and they think the whole thing is great. They have to put it to their planning committee, of course: I understand that. The councillors on the committee recognise the value of the project and are all for it, but naturally have to consult their officers. Like this man.'

He turned to pour his scorn on Arnold.

'And what happens then? We faff around for weeks. A report here. A report there. Finally, what seems to be a decision and we're heading for clear water at last. And then, because one of my subcontractors loses patience, it's all up in the air again. Arguments that have already been dispensed with get dragged out again — the bloody heritage, for God's sake! Who bloody well cares about bits of old bone in the ground, when new jobs are at stake? But the pressure is on from the media. And the council is running scared again. Well, let me put it like this. I can put pressure on too. I've invested too much time and too much money in the feasibility study — and in greasing palms — to walk away now with my tail between my legs, compromising with a half-baked plan that will considerably raise my overall costs. No, Mr Powell Frinton, this won't do. It's not acceptable. You can get back to the drawing board. The original drawing board. For me, there's no compromise. And you can tell your council and the bloody committees and your damned officials that if they think they can avoid trouble they've got another think coming. Trouble? I can give them trouble, believe me!'

After he had gone, an ashen-faced chief executive turned to Arnold. He took a deep breath. 'That was quite a display.'

Arnold agreed. He waited.

'So where do we go from here?' Powell Frinton muttered.

Arnold hesitated. 'Much depends on how committed the support for Mr Stafford is among the councillors. We have Mr Burt-Ruckley on side, I'm pretty sure: he seems to have accepted the need for compromise, though he has intimated there are certain conditions he wants to place upon archaeological digs. And I think, in terms of public attitudes, there would be support for more investigation of the site for bog burials. They raise considerable interest, particularly when the results are promulgated properly — as Dr Power seems to do so well.'

'Mr Stafford seems very determined,' Powell Frinton worried.

'He does. But in the end, what can he do, other than put pressure on the council? It seems to me this is very much a political problem. We — Miss Stannard — have come up with a compromise solution. I think it's up to Mr Stafford, now, and the council. There's not a lot more we can do.'

'I suppose not,' Powell Frinton replied. He sighed unhappily. 'All right. I suppose I'd better have a word with the leader of the council as soon as possible, to brief him on what's happening.'

Two days later, all hell broke loose on Wolfcleugh Hill.

3

Dr Ferryman ripped the rubber gloves from his hands with a slapping sound. He removed his mask and washed his hands before drying them. He inspected his ageing, heavily jowled features in the mirror with a degree of dissatisfaction and then made his way out of the forensic laboratory area to the outside room, where John Culpeper waited for him. He shook hands and grinned. 'Been a while, John. You usually send one of your minions down here to the Newcastle forensic lab. What do you call them? Liaison officers?'

'Layabouts, more like,' Culpeper grunted. 'Standing around doing nothing, waiting for you people to make up your minds about things that are already obvious to anyone with any sense and eyes in his head. If you'd only listen to us before you start the poking around—'

'An old argument, my friend, an old argument. To take suggestions from the police would be a contamination of our integrity. We need to approach our work with an open mind. We must not taint our objectivity with suggestions as to what our results should be, merely to satisfy the desires of our comrades who uphold the best traditions of the law.'

'You always did talk a lot of bollocks, Charlie Ferryman,' Culpeper said affably. 'I seen you legless on a Saturday night too often to take all that guff from you about integrity.'

'Never behind the wheel of a car, John, never that. However, let's sit down over here. You've come about the materials brought in last week, I suppose? I'm surprised it's you personally, though.'

Culpeper shrugged. 'Manpower problems. And I felt like a trip to the big city.' He flopped his heavy bulk into the worn settee that had been placed for visitors outside Dr Ferryman's office. The pathologist walked over to a coffee machine, glanced enquiringly in Culpeper's direction and, when he received a shake of the head, obtained a single paper cup of coffee. 'Probably drunk this stuff here before, have you? Wise man to decline.'

'So. The Wolfcleugh stuff.'

'Yes.' The pathologist sipped his coffee and made a wry face. 'It never improves . . . Wolfcleugh, now. First of all, as I understand it, there was a single bone found in the first instance.'

'A student, camping up there, part of the protest group.'

'Ah yes. Well, I can tell you with some conviction that there'd be no point in you spending time over that item. It's a human thigh bone, without doubt. But my guess is that it's very, *very* old. You'll remember, I imagine, when that body — they call him the Wolf Man, I believe — was discovered at Wolfcleugh Moss we advised that a police search should be made of the surrounding area.'

'Ah-huh. We excavated and sieved a hell of a lot of peat around the spot, but we didn't find anything else. And by then we'd been advised the body was old. Then the archaeological team took over, and they've come up with various artefacts and conclusions about the burial site in the old bog.'

'Yes, that would be after we got the report from the Oxford University research laboratory. They did a radiocarbon dating of the Wolf Man remains. Nothing for the police to get excited about — it all happened a long time ago. Well, in respect of this thigh bone recently discovered, we were able to run our own checks — we've got a bit more sophisticated since the Wolf Man was found — and can assure you there's nothing there for your people. The bone is probably to be dated, give or take fifty years, round about 1700 BP.'

'Which means?'

'Roman period.'

Culpeper grunted. 'That old?'

'My guess. We can get confirmation later. It's difficult to know why there was no preservation, as in other bog finds, but I would guess that the corpse might not have actually been buried immediately: wild animals had their way with him — there's some evidence of that. Stripped the bone, probably cleaned off all the flesh. So the body would have been scattered. But all before your time. And even mine.'

'Him?'

'Fairly certainly. Who knows, maybe a Roman soldier getting lost in the fog, or making back to barracks, attacked by wolves?'

'For a pathologist you have a lively mind.'

'Romantic soul, old friend.' Dr Ferryman sipped at his coffee again and frowned. 'But as for the other remains, different story. I can't be precise about this, so don't take it as read, because before I would be prepared to commit myself to paper I'd need confirmation from Oxford and maybe elsewhere, Manchester possibly. I'm making a supposition only.'

'So tell me.'

Ferryman stroked his lower lip. 'The material consisted of a foot, part of a leather shoe, and attached to the bone itself is some tissue and a strip of skin. There are elements of preservation, clearly, in the tanning of that skin, due to the properties of the peaty ground in which it was buried. But the first thing I can tell you is that it's not a recent burial. On the other hand, the nature of the scrap of leather would suggest it's of more recent origin and manufacture. It's certainly not as old as the thigh bone. Or the Wolf Man, come to that.'

'You mean we don't need to fuss over this either?'

Ferryman shook his head doubtfully. 'Probably not. You would need to search the site pretty thoroughly to find the rest of the body. And I gather—'

'The site's a mess,' Culpeper admitted. 'Bulldozers tearing around, cutting up the ground, they could have moved any other material all over the place, or buried it more deeply. We just don't have the manpower, as the Assistant Chief Constable keeps telling me. It would take a superhuman effort to mount a search.'

'And even policemen are not superhuman, hey? No, my advice would be don't waste your time on it. Unless you find something more positive on it, like more remains. Meanwhile, I'll get what we have off to Oxford so we can get a more precise dating than the one I have in my head. All I can say is, the stuff's pretty old.'

'Right.' Culpeper heaved himself to his feet with a satisfied grunt. 'So I can call off the operation. We can dismantle our tent and steal away.'

'You might be interested, however,' Ferryman added, squinting up at him, 'in what conclusions I have tentatively drawn.'

'Talk to me.'

'I would guess the foot belonged to a young woman. I would suggest her age was something between thirty and fifty. This is all tentative, of course.'

'Naturally.'

'And the other thing is, she was black. Close to it, anyway, even allowing for the tanning by the peat.' Culpeper raised his eyebrows in surprise. 'What the hell was a black woman doing around Wolfcleugh Hill years ago?'

Ferryman smiled. 'Indeed.' He sipped at his coffee. 'Who's paying for all this work, by the way?'

'Put in your invoice, Charon.'

The pathologist chuckled at the old joke. 'Have to pay the Ferryman, hey?'

Five minutes later, as he was getting into his car, the call came over his car radio telephone, and thoughts of the black woman on Wolfcleugh were banished from his head. Culpeper swore luridly and drove out of the Gosforth laboratory car park to head back north. There was a pitched battle going on at Wolfcleugh Hill.

4

'It all began early this morning,' Diane Power said helplessly. 'When we got here the madness had already started. The police began to arrive about an hour ago. I can't imagine why it took them so long, but it's been mayhem up there. Thank the Lord none of it has spilled down here.'

Arnold glanced at Portia. She was standing looking up towards the woods. She was wearing a short dark skirt and a white blouse. He guessed she must have left the office earlier than he had. He had not seen her earlier during the day. 'What time did you get here?'

She shrugged, almost sullenly. 'About an hour ago. I had to get out of that office for a while. And I'd heard Diane had had some good news.'

Dr Power nodded, but despondency was edging her mouth. 'That's right. I got a letter last night, from the British Museum and English Heritage. It said that provided we get the permission of the site owner — and I guess that's now in place after your recent meeting with Burt-Ruckley — funding for a seven-week excavation will be made available.'

'At Wolfcleugh Hill?'

Diane Power squinted up towards the woods. 'Exactly that. So old Maggie Cleugh's original funding won't be going to waste. They've given us several objectives. We are required to relate the stratigraphy of the peat block where the Wolf Man was found to the stratigraphy of the Moss overall. Secondly, we need to show the nature of the peat bog at the time of the deposition. And here's the important bit, for the future. We are to establish the changing environment of Wolfcleugh Moss throughout the last one thousand years. That means we have a legitimate case for working in Wolfcleugh Woods. And now, *this* . . .' she added despairingly.

Arnold shaded his eyes, looking up to the clamour on the hill, against the afternoon sun. Diane Power moved away towards the wooden hut. 'Hold on, I've got some binoculars here. You'll have a better view of what the idiots are up to.'

The powerful binoculars sprang the scene into sharp focus. There was a running battle going on in the woods. A number of vehicles had been parked along the verge on the south side of Wolfcleugh and it was clear that a determined attempt was being made to evict the protesters from the trees. The mayhem of the earlier bulldozer attack had resulted in the destruction of part of the campsite. This new invasion was completing the job. As he swept the binoculars along the line of sight Arnold could make out the walkways, hanging, stripped from the trees. A small fire had been started at the edge of the clearing and figures in yellow jackets were damping it down, swinging blankets at the embers. There was a single fire engine on the scene, scurrying figures manipulating a hose.

Men were still thrashing about in the undergrowth, fist fights, swinging clubs, bleeding heads, a melee of small, individual battles, the occasional group kicking at something on the ground. The police were there but vastly outnumbered and they seemed content for the moment to control the edge of the fighting, bringing out wounded young people, dragging a single kicking skinhead from the affray. The shouting came down to them from the hill, broken, disjointed, hysterical, and Arnold could make out a series of running battles taking place. At one point he thought he caught a glimpse of Nick Semmens, swinging out wildly with a pick handle against a menacing group of skinheads, but he could not be sure.

'How long has this been going on?' he asked, lowering the binoculars.

'Several hours,' Diane Power replied dejectedly. 'It seems a group of people arrived this morning, went straight into the woods and started tearing down the walkways. Over last weekend the protesting group were swollen in strength, because of the recent publicity over the bulldozers. So they were able to put up a strong resistance. But it's got quite vicious, believe me. And a couple of police cars arriving did nothing to stop it. There's a few more arrived now, but it's all a bit late. What the hell is going to happen now I can't imagine. Anyway, I'm disgusted with it all. Just when things were getting clearer, with the Heritage grant and a solid reason to settle things down. This is going to spoil everything. So, to hell with it. Let them get on with it, the stupid oafs. I've got better things to do with my time.'

She turned away, walked back towards the trench where some of the young university students she was using were standing, staring up at the mayhem on the hill. 'Come on, we've got work to do. Forget all that nonsense up there.'

Arnold took the binoculars back to the hut. When he returned to Portia he said, 'I don't think there's anything we can do here. Where's your car?'

'I came by the top road. The police had a road block there so I left it, came down to see Diane on foot.'

'I can give you a lift up to it if you like.'

She nodded despondently. She took the passenger seat and Arnold drove off the site, up the track to where she had parked her car, the far side of the police road block. He pulled in just in front of her car. 'This all right?'

She was silent for a little while. Then she glanced at him. 'I don't want to go back to the office just yet. That cow Karen . . .' She hesitated. 'Arnold, will you walk with me? On the hill.'

He thought about it for a moment, recognising the strange mood she was in. There was nothing urgent to drag him back to the office and it would be late in the day by the time he got there, anyway. He nodded. 'All right. But we'd better stay away from that battle along there.'

They got out of the car, Arnold locked it and they walked slowly up the hill, on the narrow path skirting the woods. There was the scent of honeysuckle in the air, where it clustered at the edge of the woods, and as they climbed there was a distant flash of blue from the sea, hazy, far off. The grass was high here, rustling slightly in the light breeze that came up from the coast and banks of fern lay to their left, green, waving in the soft afternoon air.

'I don't know whether I can stick it much longer, Arnold,' Portia said quietly.

He took her hand, squeezed it lightly. 'It's not that bad, is it?'

'I just feel so bloody frustrated,' she said. 'I wonder why Karen ever appointed me in the first place. I thought after a while it was done as a way of getting at you, placing me in between, stripping you of some of your authority. But it doesn't seem to be like that. Not now. Whatever she thought about me at the beginning, she seems to have changed. She's always seen you as a rival, I can see that, but now she seems to see me in the same light. She watches me, cuts me down, ignores my suggestions, and this latest thing . . . I mean, Arnold,' she went on in a sudden burst of passion, 'I worked on that report. And now she's taken it on as her own, taking the credit for it all.'

Arnold smiled in sympathy. 'I wouldn't worry about it. This recent turn of events makes it all a bit academic anyway.'

'That isn't the point, though, is it? It's her general attitude. I just don't understand it. Maybe I should get out.'

'Don't act too hastily,' Arnold advised. 'We're all under a lot of pressure right now.'

She was silent for a little while. She still clung to his hand. Hers was slim, cool to the touch. They reached the brow of the hill and Wolfcleugh Woods, dark and heavy, lay to their left. The confused sound of shouting had decreased; the echoes of violence had faded. The anger had subsided and the air was warm about them. Below them the hill sloped greenly down to the valley, bisected by the small beck across which the planning department's new road would run. There was a wisp of smoke drifting from the farmhouse way below them. Beyond, the line of the Cheviots rose, blue in the distance. Arnold doubted that the road would ever be constructed now. The whole project was at risk. If it was Ken Stafford's men who had started the riot, it was a tactic that could blow up in his face. It could mean the end of the Shangri-La development. Unless the council panicked, gave him what he wanted.

'Sometimes I think the problem is you,' Portia said quietly, as they stood there looking down into the valley.

'Sorry?' Arnold was pulled back from his own thoughts.

'Karen. I think maybe she's got it in for me because of you.'

'I don't understand.'

'Have you had an affair with her, Arnold?'

'No.'

'Never slept with her?'

'No.'

'Thought about it?'

He laughed. There had been just that one time, when they kissed after a moment of terror and violence, but it had been relief-driven, not really sexual. 'I imagine most of the department, the men that is, have thought at some time or another about sleeping with Karen Stannard. She's a beautiful woman.'

'I think she has feelings about you,' Portia said, eyeing him carefully. 'Feelings she controls to a large extent and maybe resents. She projects a certain ambivalence . . . she wants something and she resents wanting it.'

'I've not seen it.'

'Put it down to woman's intuition.'

Her fingers were linked firmly with his. They were silent for a little while and then she half-turned, moving closer to him, almost leaning against him. He looked down at her, very aware suddenly. Her olive skin was smooth perfection, her almond eyes half-lidded, her lips slightly parted and her breathing seemed to have changed. Her tone was provocative, her voice a little husky. 'That evening, when you asked me to have dinner with you. How would it have ended?'

He looked at her. His chest felt tight and his own breathing had become somewhat ragged. He made no reply.

'Would it have ended like this?' she asked and put her right hand up, behind his head, drawing him down to her mouth. Her lips were moist, soft, sweet. They held the kiss for a long time, her tongue flickering against his and then she was pulling him down gently, so that they were kneeling in the grass. Then she broke away, smiled at him almost conspiratorially. Her slim fingers crept up to her throat. 'Make it now, Arnold.'

They lay down in the long grass together, his pulses racing. She tugged at the blouse she wore and she took his hand, slipped it inside. He cupped her cool breast, stroked its softness and she sighed, wriggled, moved her body sinuously against his. Her mouth reached for his again and they were close, entwined, searching with hands and mouths. She was more practised than he had expected and her passion was quick and urgent. Her slim body was cool under his hands as they stripped each other, her eyes lidded as she kissed him, her lips on his body, his mouth on hers. The long grass moved gently in the breeze above them as, in a little while, he slipped inside her. At the first, gentle resistance to his pressure. Her dark eyes flared momentarily, and then she closed her lids and the slow, wet, sliding rhythm began. She whispered words he could not understand in his ear. Her arms clasped him tightly, dragging him closer while her dampening thighs moved with his. His senses were clouded, drugged with the essence of her. He was conscious only of her murmuring, her light moaning and the sensation in his loins as she drew him in. They moved together in a timeless rhythm until at last the world began to quicken about them, lurching, spinning with their passion until it grew dark behind his eyes and he began to lose himself, surging, almost painfully. She cried out and her body curved and bucked and strained under his. Then there was the long, slow return of reality. Sunlight and the smell of the grass.

They lay together silently for a long while. Above their heads a distant plane stitched a white edge across the deep blue of the sky. The faint sound of a tractor, working way down in the valley, formed the background to their thoughts. At last, she propped herself up on one naked elbow and stared at him. He could read nothing in her eyes; she said nothing. After a little while she sighed, pulled her body away from his and sat up, began to dress. Her breasts gleamed in the sunlight, a light sheen on her skin — the residue of their excitement. He watched her numbly.

She stood up, tucking her blouse into her skirt. She leaned forward, smiled slightly and touched him briefly on the cheek. 'I'm going down now. You stay here.'

He had no intention of moving. He lay there in the grass as she went down the hill and thought back over the years. He thought of the hills of Yorkshire where he had grown up; the long walks in the tall grass, the splendid sweep of the fells, the deep carved beauty of the dales. He remembered the time he had spent with Jane Wilson, now lost to him, married, in the States. He recalled other women he had known, years ago in his youth, and Karen Stannard's features suddenly came to him, unbidden.

He rolled over. The sun was getting lower in the sky.

He realised it was at least twenty minutes since Portia had left him. He dressed slowly. The numbness was still inside him. He was reluctant to think about what had happened here on the hill, but he could not avoid it. Their coupling had been passionate and wild, but there had been something wrong. Something missing. He thought about it now, almost dispassionately, pored over it as he sat there, and finally he stood up, looked about him. The hill seemed cooler now, the breeze on his hot face stronger.

Something missing. He knew.

What had happened — it had not been about him and Portia. It was about something else. Portia had used him: her passion had been driven by her need to relieve herself of resentment and anger. It had not been about him at all. It had all been about Karen Stannard.

He should have felt philosophical about it, but he could not. His senses were dulled, his mind confused. He started to walk back down the hill.

The woods at Wolfcleugh were quiet now. As he entered the coolness under the trees to take a quicker, more direct route down to the car he recalled the violence he had seen through Diane Power's binoculars. It seemed now as though the battle was over. The police would have taken away some of the obvious ringleaders, moved the rest of them back to their cars, forced them, persuaded them to drive away from the scene of carnage. There were still some of the protesters in the woods, he guessed, nursing their wounds. Somewhere off beyond the glade he crossed he could hear someone singing 'We Shall Overcome'. It had a sad, dispirited, hopeless tone to it.

He crossed the glade. The hill steepened here, dropping down to the area where the battle had been fought. There was smoke in the air, the odour of defeat.

No one had won here today, he considered. This had only caused more problems than before. Wild men had acted; wild decisions had been made. No one had won.

Not even Portia and himself.

He pushed on through the trees, rejecting the thoughts that were in his head. Brambles scratched at him; the path was wild and overgrown, little used. Then, ahead of him, to one side of the track, he made out what seemed to be a bundle lying in the bushes. As he drew closer he caught a glimpse of a woman's thigh, half exposed under a skirt that had ridden high. His mind caught a flash of Portia's skin; he could taste her in his mouth again, feel the slippery smooth-ness of her, and something rose in his chest, the bile of fear. It had been only half an hour ago . . .

He dropped to his knees, pulled back the bushes that shrouded the woman with one hand, while with the other he touched her wrist, felt her pulse. There was nothing. The wrist was cold. She was dead, the back of her head thick with matted blood.

For a panicked moment he had thought it was Portia, but had quickly realised he'd been wrong. Now he looked at the woman more closely and he recognised the dead girl at his feet, in spite of the massive head wounds inflicted upon her.

It was the young New Zealand student, Sally Burt.

CHAPTER FOUR

1

Steven Burt-Ruckley did not look well. There was an edginess about his manner, a nervousness in his gestures. His cheeks seemed gaunt, he looked older than his actual late forties and Culpeper was reminded of a line from an old poem — *His eyes were like hollows of madness* . . .

Burt-Ruckley was clearly taking the death of Sally Burt very badly.

Culpeper glanced around him: Wolfcleugh House was well furnished, there was plenty of money locked up in this house. Burt-Ruckley had lived here for years since his wife died, alone, minding his own business, living his own life, until a distant relative had come from the other side of the world. Perhaps to bring some light into his life, Culpeper considered. 'So when exactly did she visit you last?' he asked gently.

Burt-Ruckley's tone was hoarse with strain. 'Her visits were irregular. She had lodgings, you know, in Heaton Terrace in Newcastle. She stayed there most of the time because of her work at the university. After we met, I invited her to call at any time and she availed herself of the opportunity, usually at weekends and at end of term. She loved it up here at Wolfcleugh. It was so different from New Zealand, she told me. Up here there was a sense of history.'

'How did she first make herself known to you?' Culpeper asked curiously. 'I mean, had you been in contact with her parents in New Zealand?'

'No, no, it wasn't like that,' Burt-Ruckley shook his head. 'From what she told me, she decided to come to this country, and to the university, to get back to family roots. Her own parents were dead and once she settled in, she spent some of her spare time trying to research the family background. You see, her mother was my wife Amanda's half-sister — I don't think they were ever very close. But anyway, Sally's researches, they soon led to me, living in my isolation up here at Wolfcleugh. She wasn't a blood relative, of course, as I've explained, she was related to my dead wife.'

But he was taking her death hard, Culpeper concluded, as he saw the greyness of the man's mouth, the subdued panic in his eyes.

'You became fond of her?'

'Of course. She was a lovely person. We talked a lot, about the Burt-Ruckleys, about the past, about my wife — I never knew her mother, naturally, she had gone to New Zealand before I married Amanda — and she told me a great deal about her life in South Island. We got . . . close. And now, I feel responsible for her death.'

Culpeper observed the man closely. There was a haunted look about him and he seemed close to breakdown. 'Why would you feel that her death was your responsibility?'

Burt-Ruckley glared at his hands, willing them to be still, but the quivering was spasmodic, uncontrollable. 'Don't you see? If she had never come up here to Wolfcleugh; if I had never invited her to stay, to get to know the house and the hill; if I had never encouraged her, but left her alone to finish her course at the university, this would never have happened, and she would still have been alive.'

'I don't understand.'

'This damned Shangri-La development. The protesters in the woods. Don't you see? If she hadn't started coming to the house, she would never have gone down there. She would never have got involved. She would never have been killed.'

'It's hardly a clear line of responsibility,' Culpeper said gently. 'She was an adult. She was capable of making her own decisions.'

'But it was still a matter of opportunity,' Burt-Ruckley insisted, twisting his lean hands together. 'I thought little of it at the time, of course. In fact, it was she who first told me about Semmens and the protest. I believe she might have met him at the university, when he was canvassing support. I'm not sure about that. But when she told me there was a protest being organised I was not much interested. I live a quiet life here; some would say hedonistic. I have my expensive pleasures, but I can afford them. I have my occasional trips abroad. But I love Wolfcleugh. I'm not interested in the outside world. Wolfcleugh is my world. So at first I wanted nothing to do with the protest group. Then, well, she persuaded me. She explained what the Shangri-La development would do to the woods. She told me how Semmens might be able to stop it all. I didn't have to do anything. All I had to do was give them permission to come on to the land, build their defences.' His hollow eyes gleamed dully. 'She could be persuasive, you know. And I was fond of her. And lazy. So I gave in. I agreed they could enter the woods. I should have known better.' He hesitated, was caught up in thought for a little while. Then he said, 'It sounds now as though I'm trying to evade responsibility for her death. That it was she who persuaded me . . .'

It was beginning to sound like that to Culpeper.

'But I cannot evade such responsibility,' Burt-Ruckley announced, drawing himself up with a hint of misplaced pride. 'I allowed all this to happen. And it led to her death.'

Culpeper wrinkled his nose. He felt there was a non sequitur here somewhere. He grunted. Non sequitur: Latin, that's what came of consorting with bloody Farnsby. 'Let's get back to what I was asking earlier. You told me Sally Burt came up to Wolfcleugh irregularly. But when was her last visit?'

'Two days ago. She came here in the late afternoon. But she didn't stay.' Burt-Ruckley bared his teeth in a grimace of self-disgust. 'I should have insisted she stay. But you see, once the protest started a little while ago, although she would come up here to see me, she stayed at Wolfcleugh House less and less. She tended to go down to the woods, join the protesters overnight. She'd become friendly with them. Particularly the self-proclaimed leader.'

'Nick Semmens?' Culpeper asked, raising his eyebrows. 'She'd become friendly with him? What exactly do you mean?'

'My impression,' Burt-Ruckley replied, 'was that they had become somewhat . . . close. I didn't approve, naturally, but she was really a friend, not a blood relative, and it wasn't my business.'

'Why didn't you approve?'

'Semmens . . . I didn't think he was a very suitable person for her. I only met him once or twice — she brought him here once. He was . . . immature, irresponsible. But I got the impression she . . . perhaps infatuation is too strong a word.'

Culpeper bent over his notebook. Semmens. Something gnawed at him, an uncertainty, a feeling that something was out of place. 'So she didn't stay, the last time she called here. Why did she call?'

Burt-Ruckley shrugged. There was a faraway look in his eyes as his glance slipped past Culpeper, through the windows of the library, to the hills and the meadows in the distance. 'Just courtesy. We chatted for a while. About family. That sort of thing. She brought me up to date with her research work. Then she left.'

'To go where?'

'To the camp. She told me she was meeting Semmens. We know now it was a bad time to go down there. Next morning the violence erupted.'

And Sally Burt died.

Slowly, Culpeper closed his notebook and regarded the man seated across at the other side of the long oaken library table. 'So what do you think happened up there?'

115

Burt-Ruckley shook his head sadly. 'I don't know. Maybe she was caught up in the violence. Perhaps it was an accident. But however it happened . . .' There was a sudden flare, a glint in his eyes. 'However it happened, it will have had something to do with that man Semmens . . . But again, why should it all not be laid at the door of that dreadful man Stafford. This is all his doing, isn't it? He's determined to get his way. And it's ended with a young woman's death.' His voice was shaky with grief. And something else, Culpeper felt. But it was something he was unable to place.

Culpeper took his leave of Burt-Ruckley, told his driver to meet him on the other side of the hill and watched him as he drove away down the rasping gravelled drive. Then he turned and walked up the hill.

He wanted time to think, to look at the rounded scene. And though a fine mist, almost a sea fret, had crept inland and was shrouding Wolfcleugh Woods, it was still pleasant walking through the long grass, feeling the fresh breeze in his face, damp, clinging to the grey hairs that still remained on his head. Perhaps this was the path Sally Burt had taken up to the hill, and down through the woods to see Semmens and the other protesters. Perhaps not. Had she stayed with Semmens that night before the protest? Had she slept among the tree houses? Presumably so. He wondered again about the false note in Burt-Ruckley's voice when he spoke of Semmens. The man had not approved of Sally Burt's relationship with the leader of the protesters. Was there a hint of jealousy in the tone? There was *something* there, Culpeper was certain of it. Something that did not ring quite true.

His breathing was becoming ragged, laboured as he reached the top of the hill. Time was he could have run up here. Not now. Retirement beckoned. Physically, he wasn't the man he had been. His wife could testify to that, he thought, somewhat regretfully. But at least he still had his wits about him and experience helped . . .

He made his way down through the edge of the woods and soon discerned the police activity near the site where

Sally Burt's body had been found. Fingertip searches: in woodland like that there was little chance they would find anything significant, but it had to be done. They'd found no murder weapon so far. Not much chance of finding it either, in these woods. It could have been a thick, stubby branch of a tree. If they found it, it would have matted blood and hair, several blows had been struck, from behind. But no chance of fingerprints on the coarse bark. There might be something else, of course: flakes of skin, a chance of DNA samples. But first they had to find the dammed thing and then it would be a while before forensic came up with anything that would help along those lines.

He sighed, looked about him. She had come up here, visited Burt-Ruckley, then gone down to see her friends in the woods. Next morning the violence had begun. From here, where she had died, Culpeper could see the ravages that the battle had caused among the trees. Flattened undergrowth, trampled in the heat of the many individual battles that had occurred; burned-out trees, a general swathe of destruction. Here, the forensic team was at the edge of the battle area, looking down at the scene. So what had happened? Maybe Sally had tried to get away from the violence. Maybe she had been making her way back up the hill, possibly seeking the safety of Wolfcleugh House again when the thugs arrived.

Then, as she was scrambling up the hill, someone had come upon her from behind, struck her, sent her tumbling face down into the undergrowth, to be beaten again and again in a frenzy. What had Sally Burt done to inspire such a frenzied attack?

Culpeper shook his head. Time to leave the hill, get back to Ponteland. There were other interviews to be conducted.

* * *

Detective Inspector Farnsby was already there, waiting for him. Culpeper did not like Farnsby: he disliked his smoothness, his lean, saturnine features, the washed-out blue eyes, his

117

cool air of superiority and the fact of his accelerated promotion. He was of the graduate entry school and he seemed to think that outweighed experience, the kind of experience that had shaped Culpeper, the flash of knives in dark Tyneside alleys, dangerous doorways in Shields and drunken violence in Tyneside dockland areas. That kind of experience was worth ten university degrees, but the Assistant Chief Constable didn't seem to think so. Culpeper's lip curled. 'Nice to see you back, Farnsby. Good course down at York, was it?'

'I learned something, sir.'

'You? Thought you knew it all already.'

Farnsby did not rise to the bait. His lips thinned a little, but he jerked his head towards the interview room. 'Nick Semmens is waiting there. He was brought in about an hour ago. Wasn't happy to come.'

'Where did they find him?'

Farnsby permitted himself a wolfish grin. 'Central Station. Ticket to London. Mr Semmens was heading for the Smoke, it seems.'

Culpeper nodded. 'All right, I'll have a chat with Mr Semmens. What's happening about the Shangri-La people?'

'Mr Stafford will be coming in this afternoon. Voluntarily, it seems: he rang in, said he'd like to talk to us.'

'Interesting. We certainly want to talk to him.' Culpeper hesitated. 'But don't waste your time, Farnsby. Now that you're back doing the drudgery with me, get to those files you're so contemptuous of. This man Stafford, he's got a right-hand man called Graham, Colm Graham. I got a prickly feeling at the back of my neck about that character. I think he might be muscle. Run a computer check on him — I know you're a whizz hand at that sort of thing. Comes with a good education, don't it?'

He was pleased at the sight of the sourness of Farnsby's mouth, as he walked away to the main office. Culpeper headed for the interview room.

Semmens was waiting and seemed unhappy about it. He was not looking his best. There was a new purple swelling beneath his left eye and a long graze on his jaw. His skin seemed yellowish, dirty, and his lips were thick and bruised. He would be having some difficulty speaking, Culpeper concluded happily. He was going to enjoy prolonging this. Culpeper straddled the chair, leaning his forearms against its ladder back and staring into the unhappy, resentful eyes of Nick Semmens. 'Well, bonny lad, tell me about it.'

'What?'

'Running for the bright lights.'

'I wasn't running.'

'Bet you was running up at Wolfcleugh. All those big bad men looking for you.'

'Bastards. They came on at us without warning. Most of us were still asleep. They had pick handles. But I wasn't running,' he said defiantly. 'I got a couple of them.'

'Before you ran,' Culpeper insisted almost sleepily. 'You must have run, Nick, because there's no report from our side that you were there when the round-up started. More than a few from both sides got bundled into the waggon and given free transport from the site, but you weren't one of them. Your ponytail was in sight, though, apparently. Took off, did you?'

'We were outnumbered,' Semmens said in a sullen tone. 'And I saw no point in being picked up by you lot.'

'Avoiding the filth. I see.' Culpeper smiled. 'Of course, the boys in blue were all down below, strung out along the road. So how did you get out? I suppose you must have legged it up the hill, over the top maybe, walked down to the south side, past Wolfcleugh House.'

Nick Semmens was silent. He was thinking, watching Culpeper, his eyes were guarded. At last he shook his head. 'No. I just stayed in the woods. Kept my head down. After it was all quiet, I made my way down towards the Moss. I never went up the hill.'

Culpeper pursed his lips. 'Pity. If you had gone up there, you might have stumbled across Sally Burt's body, isn't that so?'

There was a short silence. 'I can have a lawyer if I want.'

Culpeper grinned. 'Naturally. But we're all informal here. You're helping us with our enquiries, that's all. Lawyers . . . they always suggest to me the client has something to hide.'

'I got nothing to hide.'

'Not even about Sally?'

'What do you mean?'

'What was your relationship with her?'

The silence extended this time; it seemed to gnaw at Semmens as he pondered, his mouth working, his tongue stroking his bruised lip. At last he said, 'Look, there was nothing between me and Sally Burt. I was . . . interested in her. I like women. But there was nothing; she, well—'

'I understand she came down to the camp to see you, the night before the battle started.'

Semmens's eyes widened as he contemplated the implications of the question. He shrugged diffidently. 'If you say so. But I didn't see her.'

'So she didn't stay the night in your camp?'

'No.'

'I've been told otherwise.'

'Then you've been told wrong,' Semmens retorted defiantly.

His tone was aggressive, but it contained a hint of panic.

Culpeper was suspicious. He pursed his lips thoughtfully. 'So there was nothing at all between you?'

'We talked, from time to time.' Semmens hesitated. 'And, well, I think maybe she was a bit interested, if you know what I mean. There's women all the time you know, I can't help it if they . . .' His voice trailed away uncertainly, as though he felt he was giving too much away.

'The stud, hey, Nick?' Culpeper asked sardonically. 'You don't have a regular girlfriend, then? Just play the field?'

'You could say that.' His tone was sullen, withdrawn. 'Look, I don't think I have to answer any more questions. I didn't see Sally Burt down at the campsite. I know nothing about her death. I've got nothing more to say than that.'

If he wasn't lying, Culpeper considered, he was close to it.

2

Farnsby was not entirely useless, Culpeper conceded sourly. When he got off his superior backside, he could sometimes produce results. Half an hour before the scheduled interview with Ken Stafford he came into Culpeper's office and handed him a slim file. 'I've managed to pull this out of the central computer,' Farnsby explained. 'That led me to make a few calls via the Internet—'

'The what?'

Farnsby raised a cool eyebrow. 'It's possible to get certain information that can be useful outside police files, sir. When I was at Hendon Police College—'

'Stuff the Police College! What are you trying to say?'

'There's information about Colm Graham in the police computer. But one of the websites has been able to throw up some other interesting stuff about Ken Stafford. I don't think we should give it too much credence, because the information is clearly from people who are not terribly happy about Stafford's methods and who certainly do not rank themselves among his friends, but as background . . .'

'Lemme read this stuff,' Culpeper growled.

Farnsby waited for a few moments, then asked, 'Will you want me in on the interview, sir?'

'With Stafford?' Culpeper grimaced. 'Not required, Farnsby, not required. Stafford, it seems, is to be handled with kid gloves. It'll be coffee time with the Assistant Chief Constable.'

'I see. There's something else, sir.'

'Yes?'

'I've just had the report regarding the interview with Sally Burt's landlady. She was in digs, sir, at Heaton Terrace in Newcastle.'

'That's not a crime,' Culpeper grunted.

Farnsby ignored the jibe. 'The thing is, the landlady's made a statement to the effect that someone had been making enquiries about Sally Burt, shortly before she died.'

Culpeper's head came up slowly. 'What do you mean, enquiries?'

'Just that. Someone — a man — called at the lodgings when the girl was out, asked a few questions. The landlady directed him to the university, because Sally was out. And it seems he called at the university office later. The girl at reception there, she described him as being a bit seedy.'

'Ill-fed, was he?' Culpeper scowled.

'Interesting thing is, he left a calling card.'

'A what?' Culpeper frowned. 'He's making enquiries about Sally Burt and he leaves a calling card? What was he — someone telling her she's won a prize on the lottery?'

'No, sir. The name on the card is Dickson. Private investigator.'

'Now what the hell would *that* be all about?' Culpeper stared at the younger officer. He was obviously keen to follow through on this one and Culpeper had plenty on his plate. He sighed. 'All right, Farnsby, this one's over to you. Chase it up, find out what it's about, but damned if I can see where it leads . . .'

* * *

At two o'clock precisely Culpeper presented himself at the Assistant Chief Constable's office. Ken Stafford was already there, seemingly at ease in the chair in front of Greyson's desk. They were both smiling; some country club anecdote, Culpeper had no doubt. All very chummy.

'Ah, Culpeper, come in. Take a seat. Have you met Mr Stafford? He's come in voluntarily — not to make a statement, you understand—' Both men laughed.

Culpeper managed a smile. He sat down, the manila file tucked under his arm. 'So why have you come in, sir, may I ask?' he began immediately. The Assistant Chief Constable was not pleased; he glared at Culpeper, annoyed that a degree of coolness had entered the room with Culpeper's presence.

Ken Stafford remained at ease. He smoothed a hand down his thigh, almost absent-mindedly. 'It seemed to me that in the circumstances it would be best if I came along to help in any way I can.'

'Did you know the dead girl, then?'

Stafford looked at Culpeper, not pleased with his tone. 'I did not.'

'So how do you feel you can help?'

Stafford expelled his breath slowly, glancing at Greyson as though for assistance and guidance in dealing with the truculence displayed by his questioner.

The Assistant Chief Constable placed his fingertips together and lowered his head. 'Culpeper, Mr Stafford thought that since the girl was killed on Wolfcleugh Hill, when there was a demonstration going on down below involving protesters against a legitimate scheme that had the approval of the council . . .'

'He thought he'd come in to explain that it was nothing at all to do with him,' Culpeper interrupted.

Stafford turned his head slowly; his eyes were cold and hard. 'That's exactly it. I didn't know the girl. I'm not involved—'

'Involved?' Culpeper opened the file, placed it on his knee, inspected it with exaggerated care. 'You and Colm Graham go way back, I believe?'

There was a short silence. 'I don't see how my relationship with Graham has anything to do with this.'

'Way back . . .' Culpeper mused. 'Did you know he once did a short stretch in prison? Wonder if you knew him then? And was he with your company when that trouble started down in Blackheath? And then there was that bit of business in Nottingham . . . Where exactly do you base your headquarters, Mr Stafford? You seem to have had projects all over the place during this last fifteen years.'

'I've been pretty busy, yes,' Stafford replied coolly, but his eyes were watchful.

'Culpeper, what's this all about?' the Assistant Chief Constable asked edgily.

Culpeper ignored him. 'How is business, Mr Stafford?'

'Like life, it has its ups and downs.'

'According to some friends of yours on the Internet, it's more down than up at the moment.'

There was a short, cold silence. 'If you're referring to the people I think you are, the anonymous individuals who place so-called information on the web, they're hardly friends of mine.'

'But they have a real sense of grievance, it seems.'

'Culpeper—' There was a warning note in the Assistant Chief Constable's voice. 'Is this taking us anywhere?'

'Ah, it's all right, sir, I was just trying to get some background on Mr Stafford before we heard what he has to say about the events surrounding Miss Sally Burt's death. You see, sir, it seems that Mr Stafford — along with Mr Colm Graham, who seems to have been a right tearaway in his time and maybe still has not reached years of discretion — has been in this kind of situation before. A number of his business ventures have provoked stiff local opposition of one kind or another and all seem to have been resolved with, shall we say, a bit of muscle? Mr Graham's name has popped up from time to time, nothing proved to the satisfaction of the courts, although actions have been brought, then mysteriously dropped . . .'

'Rumours, Mr Culpeper, rumours,' Stafford said coldly. 'In any business, there are people who feel they've been—'

'Cheated? Coerced?' Culpeper smiled generously. 'I'm sure that's the case and I'm sure they're all misled in their attitudes. But trouble seems to follow you and Mr Graham, doesn't it? And then there's the web site . . .'

'I don't think—'

'Your friends there, who post their information, they reckon your company is in financial trouble, Mr Stafford. They reckon your share prices are being held up by some wheeling and dealing of a somewhat doubtful provenance. And there's the suggestion that all is not well in your little empire.'

'I haven't come in here to discuss my business affairs,' Stafford said, injecting a level of indignation into his voice. 'I came here—'

'To deny that you had anything to do with the first bulldozer attack on the camp at Wolfcleugh.'

'That was the action of a frustrated subcontractor of mine, who wanted to get things resolved—'

'And it was nothing to do with you,' Culpeper interrupted complacently. 'And this second attack, that also was nothing to do with you. The fact that a number of the people who have been arrested seem to have been employed by you from time to time, as labourers, as drivers, is irrelevant. It was all nothing to do with you. The fact that you've been getting frustrated by the delays to your project, by the failure of the council to come out with a decision, by the continued presence of the protesters at the camp, is neither here nor there. You sit back patiently and wait for the right thing to be done. You didn't send Colm Graham with his thugs into the woods; you didn't ask Colm Graham to enlist the bully boys from the National Front; you had nothing to do with the attack on sleeping men and women in the tree houses and tents at Wolfcleugh. And when, in the middle of the battle, Sally Burt got struck down and killed . . . well, that was all nothing to do with you, was it, Mr Stafford?' He smiled blandly, glancing from Stafford to the Assistant Chief Constable and back again. 'So what was it you came in to tell us, sir? How can you help our investigation?'

3

Arnold Landon was aware that currents of rumour washed around the department but no one spoke to him, or asked him about his discovery of the body of Sally Burt. It was as though they wanted nothing to do with it, afraid of some guilt by association, although he had nothing to feel guilty about in respect of the dead girl.

And yet he felt an odd sense of guilt about that day as a whole. He had seen Portia on several occasions at the office, but she had seemed as normal: efficient, friendly, self-assured, beautiful. Her eyes when she spoke to him were serene, her attitude sober. She made no reference to what had happened between them on the hill and it was as though she had erased it from her mind as something ephemeral and unimportant.

He could not treat the incident in the same way. It had left him confused. From time to time, half dreaming at his desk, he caught glimpses in his mind's eyes of the smooth contours of her breasts; he tasted her again on his lips: caught the subtle, intimate odour of her flesh in his nostrils; but he did not know how to react to her coolness. He had recognised, almost as soon as their passion had been exhausted that day, that there was no permanency to it. It had been an urgent drive fuelled by emotions that had nothing to do with their attraction to each other — rather, a complex web of resentment and frustration had thrown Portia Tyrrel to him.

And, confusingly, the whole thing was now overlaid by the sight of the dead girl, sprawled in the undergrowth, her head a mass of matted blood . . .

He had discussed the death of Sally Burt with Karen Stannard, of course, in Portia's presence. They had both shown him sympathy, realising the shock it had been for him. There had been nothing in Portia's eyes to hint at any thoughts she might have had about his finding the dead girl so soon after she and Arnold had made love on the hill. Karen, slim fingers stroking her tanned throat had said silkily, 'Of course, Arnold, if you want to take some time off . . .'

'No, that won't be necessary.'

'Then some time out of the office. Not the dig at Wolfcleugh, of course, that would be too close to recent events . . .' Arnold could not prevent his instinctive glance in Portia's direction: she remained impassive, hands folded demurely in her lap, but Karen Stannard caught the glance and paused. She looked at Portia and something moved deep in her eyes. 'I think what we could do,' she went on, 'is have Portia handle some of your office files. Then you get up north, visit the Black Moor site, finish that report that's been waiting for several weeks now, forget about bog bodies and Wolfcleugh Woods . . .' The colour of her eyes seemed to have changed again, the warmth of her sympathy being replaced by a cool blue suspicion.

Portia nodded quietly. 'I'll be happy to take over some of Arnold's work, for the time being,' she said. 'I'm sure I can handle everything he's got . . .'

Karen glanced at her sharply, suspicious. Arnold was glad to escape.

It meant that for the next few days he was able to drive into the rugged-edged hills, past banks of beech woodland and stately pines. He crossed deep burns, deliberately taking circuitous routes north, and on the high fells passed the old remnants of Victorian mine workings, abandoned now to black foxes and wild deer. On far hilltops he caught glimpses of pele towers and ruined castles; on the fell tops the wind was keen, and when the sea fret came the land was a wild and gloomy place. But he had seen it in all its seasons and moods and as he drove north he was exhilarated, his spirit lifted again.

Until the evening, taking a lonely dinner in a small hotel, deep in the Black Moor, when there was time again to think, and to see the dead girl, and to attempt to remove the images once more by walking at the riverside where the oak and birch marched up the dark hillside under a bright moon.

The Roman site had been home to the sixth legion.

Wood, clay and stone remains were being carefully excavated. The team had found a rubbish pit that was producing a rich harvest: leather shoes, coins, pins, an eagle-sculpted stone, an ornamental belt buckle in the shape of a dolphin. He discussed the finds with the team, made notes and worked them up in the evening at the hotel while the others were drinking in the bar. He seemed to have lost the appetite for socialising: the horror of finding the dead girl painfully juxtaposed with the memory, the feel, the sensation of Portia.

He could have made his way back to Morpeth on the Friday night but decided against it. He felt unable to face going home to finish the report, though there was no rational explanation for it. He merely felt that he wanted to stay up here among the wild fells, do a little work, a certain amount of thinking.

Everything was completed by mid-morning on Saturday apart from a few matters he would need to research: an hour in the library at Newcastle would sort that out on Monday. He left the hotel and walked down into the valley, to the banks of the river. He crossed the rickety old wooden footbridge, noting the collapsed stone of the Roman way some fifty yards upriver. It had been a cunningly chosen site, not the obvious and simplest one, but a site easily defended. The Romans had always been on the watch for danger, here in the wild country in the shadow of the great wall of Hadrian.

Nothing was left to chance: moats, walls, river crossings, all placed to protect the legions and their camp followers — merchants, women, slaves — from surprise attack. He sat down on the bank and the sun was warm on his back. The stream eddied in front of him, a deep pool, shadowed under the bracken, dark and cool, disturbed occasionally by the flick of quick, darting young trout, black in the smooth water.

He had no idea how long he had been sitting there, his mind empty, when he felt rather than heard the shivering of the footbridge. He looked up and saw the burly, slow-moving form of someone he knew. The man's presence was not welcome, but somehow Arnold was not surprised to see him.

Detective Chief Inspector Culpeper stood immediately behind Arnold for a little while, his shadow across the grassy bank, just touching the stream. Then with a sigh, he lowered himself ponderously, to sit uncomfortably beside Arnold. 'They told me up at the hotel you'd probably come down here. You're a hard man to find, losing yourself up here. But I can understand why you do it.'

'My job brings me up here,' Arnold said quietly.

'Fortunately, so does mine,' Culpeper replied. He snapped a blade of long grass, sucked at it between his teeth. 'Well, I suppose, strictly speaking, it shouldn't do. I could have dragged you in for a chat, or met you in the office. But I heard you were on site up here and thought I'd grab the chance for some clean air, too. Freshen up the tubes, scrub away at the old brain cells. I'm going round in circles, Mr Landon.'

Arnold made no reply. He was reluctant to think of that afternoon on the hill.

'Do you have any thoughts about Wolfcleugh? Any feelings about it?' Culpeper asked after a little while. There was a certain reluctance in his tone that surprised Arnold.

'How do you mean?'

'I don't know. It's an old place, isn't it? It's seen a lot. Bit grim, really And then there's the Moss. The old stories. I wonder just how many bodies have ended up in that ancient bog. Maybe it is just old stories. But I get a feeling about the place. Huh . . . I'm getting fanciful in my old age, but that bloody place just feels . . . evil.' He grunted. 'Coppers don't usually talk about things being evil. We're too pragmatic a bunch.' *Pragmatic.* Bloody Farnsby again.

'You came up here looking for me?'

'And to clear my head.' Culpeper grubbed for a stone near his hand, found one and tossed it into the pool. The splash frightened something downstream and there was a whirring of wings. Duck, probably, Arnold guessed.

'I've read your statement, but in view of information that's come to me since, I thought we should go over it again,' Culpeper explained. 'Clear up a few things . . . For instance, you'd met Sally Burt, knew her.'

'Not well.'

'But there was an incident when you were present, at a pub in Newcastle.'

'That's right. At the Northumberland Arms.'

'A fight, between Nick Semmens and a man called Joe Farley. You were a bit vague about the reason for the skirmish. You spoke to Sally Burt afterwards . . . took her back to her lodgings.'

'Yes.' Arnold hesitated. 'Sally had come into the pub with Semmens. But I don't know what started the fight.'

'But you can guess?'

Reluctantly Arnold said, 'It could be that Farley was angry with Semmens because of the delay to the road-building scheme.'

'Nothing more personal? Like the fact that Semmens was in the pub with Sally Burt?'

Arnold was silent for a little while. Then, mentally, he shrugged. There was no reason now why he should not explain more fully. Sally was dead. It could not hurt her. 'Sally seemed to think it might have been personal as well as over the road-building thing. Joe Farley might have been angry because of the fact that Semmens had been living with his daughter, Jenny — and had dragged her into the protest group. And now he was with Sally Burt. Sally said Farley had referred to her as a whore.'

Almost dreamily, Culpeper picked up another stone and cast it into the pool watched the ripples spread. 'Ah-huh . . . That kind of confirms what we've already got from Farley himself. But I just have the feeling there was something more.'

Arnold hesitated. 'Sally . . . Sally didn't think he knew that his daughter was pregnant by Semmens.'

'Now is that right?' Culpeper breathed. He didn't speak for a bit. Then he stirred himself and looked sideways at Arnold. 'Farley told us nothing about that. Maybe he still doesn't know. The again . . .' He was silent for a while. Then he went on, 'Burt-Ruckley says Sally Burt came to see him that evening and then went down to the camp. He suggested she slept down there, maybe with Nick Semmens, that night, the night before she died. But Semmens, he reckons he didn't see her at the camp that evening. He was around there, but . . . he claims he didn't see her. On the other hand, she was certainly there . . . and we are told by some of the other happy campers that there was an argument that evening.'

'Between whom?'

'Sally Burt and Jenny Farley. We've spoken to the Farley girl. She says it was a spat about Nick Semmens. Who she's not terribly pleased with. First, because she thinks he'd been making eyes at Sally. Second, because friend Semmens seems more than keen to get the hell out of Wolfcleugh, the north and Jenny's life.' He sighed theatrically. 'The perils of prospective parenthood, I guess.' He was rather pleased with that alliteration and smiled.

'So what hypothesis are you now constructing?' Arnold asked.

'Hypothesis?' Culpeper laughed. 'Hell, nothing like that, not yet. But I'm wondering . . . what if Joe Farley had found out his daughter was pregnant and Semmens had taken a fancy to Sally Burt? Would that be enough to make him lose his temper and clobber the rival? We know he can be a

131

violent man. Or maybe it was the quarrel in the woods that was the spark. Has young Jenny got enough of her father's genes to batter the hell out of Semmens's new love?'

'I don't think there was anything other than friendship between Sally and Semmens,' Arnold offered. Though things could change quickly, he considered to himself, as he remembered the long grass on the hill.

It was almost as though Culpeper was musing to himself aloud. 'Love triangle, girl does it, or father does it. Could have been an accident, in all that violence . . . Tell me, Mr Landon, when you found the dead girl up there, were there any signs of disturbance round about?'

Arnold shook his head. 'If you mean did the battle occur around there, no. I mean, I found her some distance above the actual campsite, where all the skirmishing took place.'

'So you don't think she was actually involved in the fighting.' Culpeper nodded. 'But round about . . . no other signs you noticed?'

Arnold shook his head slowly. 'Not that I noticed. But I'm not expert at such things. I'm no woodsman.'

'Neither are the clodhoppers who came on the scene to start with. We always warn them to treat a murder scene with respect: evidence can easily get destroyed. But there's always some idiot starts poking around before forensic get there . . .'

'Why are you asking me? Was there something I missed? Something I should have seen up there?'

Culpeper shrugged. He snapped a couple of blades of grass, held them clamped between his fingers and blew. The harsh screeching sound that emerged finally flushed the last of the duck from the river. They soared, wheeled in the sky, as Culpeper blew again. 'Always used to do that as a kid. Haven't done it for years now. Old pleasures. The fact is, Sally Burt wasn't killed where you found her.'

'What?'

Calmly, Culpeper said, 'The labs tell us she was killed somewhere else and brought down, or thrown down to where you found her. Dr Ferryman, he's pretty certain about that.

So she could have been clobbered down in the camp. Or she could have been killed up on the hill and dragged down into the undergrowth. He's still checking on things, is Dr Ferryman. Though quite where it takes us, I'm not sure. But we do know that Nick Semmens was on that hill, Jenny Farley was in the camp, and there was a sighting of Joe Farley up there too, coming back with the rest of Stafford's henchmen to finish off the job he'd started with his bloody bulldozers.'

'So there's the possibility that she was killed by accident, maybe, during the fighting on the main site.'

Culpeper thrust out a thoughtful lower lip. 'It had occurred to me. That she was killed there in the general fracas. And then dragged up away from it all, to hide the body. But Charon knocked that on the head.'

'Charon?'

'The Ferryman. My little joke. No, the good doctor tells me that wasn't possible. He's still to come out with a precise time, but he tells me that all the signs suggest that Sally Burt wasn't killed in the fighting. She actually died some hours *before* the battle started. When Stafford's thugs moved on to site she was already dead up on the hill.'

Arnold was silent. He cast his mind back, in view of what Culpeper had told him, to consider what signs of disturbance there might have been near her body. But he could recall nothing, he had not been looking for any such signs. He cast about in his mind for anything else he might be able to tell Culpeper that might help in his quest for the person who had murdered Sally Burt.

'There was another thing,' he blurted out suddenly. 'Sally was being followed . . . or at least, someone was making enquiries about her.'

Culpeper seemed preoccupied. 'A man called Dickson?' When Arnold nodded, he said, 'Yes, we've heard about that. We've got a trace out on him at the moment. Wolfcleugh. Even the name gives me the shudders and on a beautiful day like this. All those bodies, all those bones. By the way, Dr Ferryman told me the thigh bone that camper found is very old. Very old. But the foot your colleague . . . what's her name? The Chinese girl.'

'Portia Tyrrel,' Arnold replied evenly. The name seemed strange on his tongue. 'She's not Chinese. Her father is a Scot, her mother is Singaporean.'

'Whatever. Portia. Beautiful girl . . . anyway, that foot she found, it's giving Dr Ferryman considerable trouble.'

'It wasn't a recent burial,' Arnold averred. 'From my experience—'

'That's right. Not recent. Pretty old. But not that old. And black.' He squinted at Arnold reflectively. 'Fancy that. A black woman. Buried years ago in Wolfcleugh Woods.'

'You mean the Moss.'

'No. The woods. I said the remains were old. But they weren't *that* old. Dr Ferryman, he reckons it happened maybe twenty, thirty years ago. But the circumstances . . . who can tell now? When it comes down to it all we've got is a foot. The rest of her? After the bulldozers and the pitched battle, her bits and pieces could be anywhere. I think it's one dead secret Wolfcleugh will be keeping to itself for eternity . . .'

CHAPTER FIVE

1

Arnold left the high fells shortly after midday, checking out of the hotel and driving south along roads mercifully free of traffic. The discussion with Culpeper had left him vaguely unsettled. He checked his watch. He was reluctant to go straight home, so he took the A1 south to Newcastle, bypassing Morpeth. The report on the Roman site at Black Moor was all but finished. Rather than leave the thing until Monday, he would just about have time to call in at the Newcastle library, pick up the references he needed, and he could then finish the whole thing and drop it on Karen Stannard's desk first thing on Monday morning.

It would keep his mind off Sally Burt and Portia: work was the palliative.

He arrived at the city and was fortunate to find a parking place. Had Newcastle United being playing he would have stood no chance, but this was out of season and cricket on the Town Moor did not raise the same crowds. He made his way to the City Library, and spoke to the librarian, who knew him well enough and arranged for some leather-bound volumes to be brought to one of the carrels there. He walked into the stack room and in a little while he was absorbed in the research he needed to carry out on the Black Moor site.

At five he was finished. He left the materials where they were: the staff preferred it that way. He gathered up his papers and as he approached the security door leading back into the main reference room he heard someone call his name. He turned.

It was Georgina Hope, the mousy little librarian from the university library.

'Mr Landon,' she gushed. 'How nice to see you again.'

'Miss Hope. Not enough volumes in your own library?'

She giggled. 'Oh, collections can sometimes be a bit eclectic, you know. I often use the Literary and Philosophic library as well, in fact, near Central Station, because they have holdings there that are, shall we say, idiosyncratic, somewhat different from both the university and the public library. And you?'

Arnold smiled. 'I've been working on the Roman site at Black Moor. There are some Victorian research papers they hold here. I imagine they might be duplicated at the university, but I know my way around here rather better.'

'Well, you know you'll always be welcome to call in to see us.' Miss Georgina Hope proceeded primly past him as he opened the door for her to go out into the main library. He nodded to the girl at the desk and was making his way towards the stairs when he realised that Georgina Hope was waiting for him at the exit. He joined her, smiled. She had a worried frown. 'Mr Landon, it's remiss of me, but I . . . didn't mention how distressed I was to hear about the . . . death of Miss Burt.'

He nodded, his lips tightening.

'I am aware you knew her,' the little librarian said miserably, 'so please extend my sympathies to Miss Tyrrel as well. I was very unhappy to hear . . .' She was suddenly covered in confusion. 'However, I'm glad I met you now, because I haven't known quite what to do. I mean, I don't know the family and so on . . .'

'I don't believe there is any immediate family,' Arnold explained.

'Well, I don't know . . .' Her voice trailed away uncertainly. 'You see, Miss Burt spent quite a bit of time in the university library. She conducted her general research there . . . and the whole of the faculty are devastated, believe me. But I have been wondering what to do with the papers she left.'

Arnold grimaced sympathetically. 'I don't think there's anything to be done with them, really. Maybe there's something the university can use, from her research material. Otherwise, I imagine they can be disposed of.'

Miss Hope was uneasy. 'Well, the problem is, I think that it wasn't just academic research she was doing, you see. I think there was some personal material there also. I don't quite know . . . she had a locker in the department and of course, now she's . . . gone, well, we'll need to clear the material she left there. I was wondering if you . . .'

'Personal?' Arnold frowned. 'I don't know whether I'm the right person to deal with it. I hardly knew her—'

'But you are acquainted with some of her family?'

'Not really. As I said, there's no immediate family, though there is Mr Burt-Ruckley.'

'At Wolfcleugh.' Miss Hope nodded vigorously. 'That did occur to me. I mean, she used to stay with him, visit him, talk about him a little as her nearest contact in the family. Do you think . . . well would it be possible that the materials she left should sensibly be given to him? The trouble is, I don't know him and coming out of the blue, at such a sensitive time . . . he must be devastated, poor man. And I wouldn't want to intrude on his grief.'

'You'd like me to get them to him?' Arnold asked, understanding her nervousness, her fear at intrusion. 'Oh, I'd be so grateful. Do you have time to collect them now? I have the files stacked available and then we can release the use of the locker . . . I'd be so grateful . . .'

Arnold walked across through the town centre, escorting the little librarian back to the university. She trotted along beside him, relieved, happy, garrulous, but every few minutes she would lapse into apologies, aware that about them loomed the spectre of the death of a young woman they had both known and liked. They entered the library; she asked him to wait for a few minutes while she went up to get a key for the lockers. When she returned she was carrying a small box file. 'It's not a great deal,' she said, 'and I'm afraid the spring on the box cover isn't all that efficient.'

He accepted the burden. 'I'll make sure that Mr Burt-Ruckley receives it. He'll know what to do with it, I'm sure.' But he was aware that since Burt-Ruckley was not in touch with any branch of the family the personal materials belonging to Sally Burt would eventually be destined for oblivion. There was also the thought of the distress the papers might bring to Burt-Ruckley, reminding him of Sally. He had clearly been greatly upset by her death. Perhaps it would be better for him if he were not to see the box and its contents. But that was not a decision Arnold could make.

He said goodbye to Miss Hope and carried the box file back across town to his car. He put it on the passenger seat and drove out on the road home to Morpeth. It was almost six o'clock. He'd be back at his bungalow by six-thirty: a drink, something to eat, maybe watch some television.

Some idiot braked hard at the lights ahead of him. He slammed on his own brakes and came to a violent halt. The box file shot off the seat, cannoned into the glove compartment and fell into the well in front of the passenger seat.' The lights ahead were red. Swearing to himself, Arnold released his constricting seat belt, leaned over, shuffled the papers that had fallen out of the box and replaced them in the file. One of the papers was a photocopy of an old newspaper file. He saw the headline: *HAVE YOU SEEN THIS WOMAN?* He had no time to read more: the lights changed and he drove north.

After a while, curious, he glanced again at the open box file. The photocopy was still partly visible. There was a photograph under the heading: a poor reproduction of a poor original. Probably taken from a passport. The face was that of a young woman: staring eyes, long black hair, slightly parted mouth. She was black.

Arnold wondered why Sally Burt would be undertaking private research which would involve cuttings from an old newspaper with a picture of a young black woman. At the next set of lights he flopped the box file closed, so that papers would no longer go flying around if he braked again.

The late afternoon sun gleamed on the hills as headed north, home to Morpeth.

When he drove into the quiet cul-de-sac where he lived, he was surprised to see there was a car parked outside his door, its engine running impatiently. It was a red Toyota Celica. He pulled into the driveway and got out. The driver of the car behind him did not.

The electric window of the Toyota whirred down.

Karen Stannard sat there, glaring at him. 'About time! Where the hell have you been?' she snapped.

'You know where I've been. Up at Black Moor. At the Roman site.'

'You left there hours ago.'

There was no point in discussing it. 'What's the problem?'

'I've been trying to contact you since this morning. There's been no answer from your mobile phone.'

'I've had it switched off. Saving electricity.'

She was not amused. 'You got a dinner jacket?'

'Yes.'

'I'll be back in an hour. Be ready.' She gunned the engine, began to back away.

'Hold on,' he called. 'What's this about?'

'Dinner, seven-thirty tonight.'

'But I—'

'There'll be a taxi, at seven-fifteen. You make sure you're ready. I need an escort to the dinner. You're it.'

With a gusty roar the Toyota was away down the road, out of the cul-de-sac. When Karen Stannard was in such an imperious mood there was no gainsaying her. Arnold was left with an hour to shower and change.

* * *

The dinner was held in the Gosforth Park Hotel, near the racecourse. There were perhaps a hundred and fifty people there, most of the great and the good of Tyneside. There were a few young people present, probably young professionals who had come on family invitations, but the company was mainly middle-aged and self-satisfied, the speeches boring and repetitive, the dinner excellent. Arnold quite enjoyed himself, not least because he was amused by the manner in which many of the middle-aged men clearly envied him his companion.

Karen looked superb. She wore a black evening dress, low cut to reveal her splendid throat and more than a hint of her equally splendid bosom. She was in sparkling form: her eyes were bright, her conversation anima ted as they moved on the fringes of the pre-dinner cocktail groups, and she seemed to know quite a number of the people present. She had explained the situation in the taxi, on the way to the dinner. 'It's a political thing, really. My escort was supposed to be Councillor Jonson, you know, chairman of the Environmental Committee, but he rang this morning to say he was indisposed. I think it was his hag of a wife, really: when she heard he was escorting me, she put her foot down.' She'd given Arnold a sideways glance. 'I can't imagine why I inspire such nervousness in wives.'

He understood it completely.

At dinner she said very little to him, but did press upon him that he was to use her first name. 'I don't want any Miss Stannard nonsense on a social occasion such as this,' she warned him. But he had very little opportunity for conversation with her. The deputy leader of the council was on her left and he paid her meticulous attention. She glittered and sparkled at him so he got full value for his sedulousness, but Arnold suspected from the grim line of his wife's mouth that he might pay for it later, in the drawing down of the evening.

Powell Frinton was also there; his wife was dumpy and lacked dress sense. There were several other senior officers present; they seemed somewhat surprised to see Arnold, but quickly appeared to realise he was standing in for someone else with the delectable Karen Stannard. So they tended to ignore him, both pre-dinner at cocktails and later, when brandy and coffee were served in the outer lounge. Arnold soon got separated from Karen, as she butterflied around the room, and found himself able to stand in a corner near the window leaning against the wall, sipping a brandy and contemplating the gathering with a jaundiced eye.

It was there that Karen Stannard found him, just before eleven o'clock. 'Right,' she said. 'Duty done. Let's get away before the groping starts.'

She had clearly imbibed well. There was the glint of malicious amusement in her eyes. He looked around, convinced she was exaggerating the dangers to her person, since most of the men there were accompanied by their watchful wives She must have caught the doubt in his eyes. She shook her head, smiling at him. 'Don't doubt me. You wouldn't believe the kind of chances they'll take. Even under the eagle eyes of their spouses.'

They had no problem obtaining a taxi outside the hotel. Karen Stannard was quiet when they drove back towards her apartment. She seemed to withdraw into a corner of the seat, as though avoiding contact with him. Accordingly, he was somewhat surprised when they arrived at the block of flats where she had her home. 'Pay the driver,' she said. 'Then come up for a black coffee.'

He did as he was ordered.

The flat was tastefully decorated and furnished. She did not ask him if he wanted something stronger than coffee. She merely poured him a stiff brandy, placed it on the low table in front of him as he sat on the settee and went into the kitchen to make the coffee. Arnold sniffed at the cognac: it was expensive.

Karen came back in with the coffee, placed the small tray on the table between them. She poured herself a brandy and sat in the easy chair opposite him. She sipped her drink, watching him over the rim of the glass. Her eyes seemed to be a deep violet in colour, a hint of amusement lurking in their depths. 'Would you be surprised if I told you that you were the first man to have come into this place?'

'I suppose I would be.'

'It's not that they haven't tried. But this is my . . . hideaway.'

'Have you much to hide from?'

She laughed. 'The world, on occasions. The job can be stressful, as you know. And then, there are always men . . .' She observed him carefully, drew her legs up under her. The long skirt opened, revealing the length of her elegant calf. 'What do you think of me, Arnold, as a woman?'

She was tall, slim-hipped, deep-breasted and she was possibly the most beautiful woman he had known. Her eyes had the capacity to change colour in accordance with her mood; her features were classical, her mouth wide and occasionally generous. Her hair held glints, natural lights that were sometimes auburn, sometimes red. 'I try not to think about it,' he lied.

She knew it and smiled. 'I wonder why it is that you're the only man in the department who hasn't lusted after me and shown it. Is it something to do with you?'

'I'm normal enough.'

'The rumour is I'm not.' She showed her teeth in a grimace. 'Oh, don't look so worried. I'm well aware that various people have commented that they consider me to have lesbian tendencies. But that's all it is, Arnold. Rumour.'

'I'm sure that's so.'

She regarded him soberly then leaned forward to pour the coffee. The neck of her dress fell forward and he could see the swell of her breast. He sipped his cognac; he was feeling warm.

She leaned back in her chair again. 'What do you think of Portia?'

It was a dangerous question. He hesitated. 'She's a colleague whose judgement I respect. She works hard. She's committed. She's got a mind of her own.'

'You choose your words with care, Arnold. And you didn't mention the fact that she's a very attractive woman.' She raised an interrogative, perfectly arched eyebrow. 'So do you want to tell me what's going on?'

'In what respect?'

'You and Portia.'

'I don't know what you're talking about.'

She was unconvinced, aware of his prevarication. He felt uncomfortable.

'How long have we been working together now, Arnold? Must be all of five years, I would guess.'

'About that,' he agreed.

'You can't work with someone that long, and work closely together, and not be aware when things have changed. And I believe they have, in a subtle way I can't yet pin down.'

He was silent. She sipped at her brandy, watching him, like a cat curled up in the chair, sleepy-eyed, yet contemplative, wary. 'I've become aware of a sort of . . . atmosphere in the office during the last few days. Portia, well, she's Portia, controlled, giving nothing away. But you . . . you've been uneasy, Arnold. And I have a feeling it's something to do with Portia. The way you've looked at her, once or twice. And you're not easy in her presence. So tell me, what's happened?'

'You're imagining things,' he insisted.

'Are you two sleeping together?' There was something odd about her tone. She clearly wanted the question to come out steadily, a casual question, one that was of no great moment to her. But she was betrayed by an underlying tone, a slight shakiness which could have been concern, or annoyance. Or jealousy.

Arnold stood up. He finished his cognac and looked down at her. 'We are not sleeping together.' They had made love, he argued silently to himself, but that did not imply they had now developed an ongoing relationship. 'It's getting late. I'd better go.'

She put down her own drink. The coffee on the table lay untouched. She preceded him to the door. She turned and faced him. 'I suppose I should thank you,' she said demurely, 'for indulging me at such short notice, escorting me to the dinner.'

'I enjoyed it.'

'So did I. Anyway, by way of thanks . . .' She stood close to him, put her arm round his neck and kissed him. For a moment it was simply warm and friendly, but then, almost unconsciously they both allowed it to turn into something else. He drew her closer, the touch of their bodies became electric and they stood there for a long while, pulses racing, until she drew back from him, looked at him long and hard. Then she broke away, opened the door. 'I enjoyed that, too. Think about that, if you ever do get ideas about Portia.' Her smile was supposed to be cynical, but it was shaky at the edges. 'But don't read too much into it. I only wanted to prove to you that sex and the office — they just don't go together.'

2

On Monday morning in the office Arnold felt unsettled. He tried to concentrate on the files on his desk, but his mind kept wandering. He had seen neither Karen nor Portia and he wanted to see neither, but Karen Stannard's last words to him drummed consistently in his head. And it was foolish to think that he could possibly avoid seeing them in the office. The trouble was, he could not even be certain that the two women had not discussed him among themselves. He doubted it, because there was a certain cool hostility between Karen Stannard and her assistant these days. But in the confusion of his mind, he felt anything was possible.

At midday, to his surprise, Karen Stannard came to his office. She was her usual cool, elegant, controlled self. She wore a dark-grey business suit that set off her figure to perfection. 'Arnold,' she said casually, 'I assume you've finished the report on the Black Moor site.'

'It's here.'

'I have a meeting with the Heritage people over lunch. I'll take the file with me.'

And the credit, he thought.

She glanced over his desk and saw the box file that he had brought in with him. 'What's this?'

Arnold hesitated. 'It's some private papers that belonged to Sally Burt. She'd left them in a locker at the university library.'

'So why are they here?' Karen queried, raising an eyebrow and opening the box lid with feline curiosity.

'Miss Hope — the librarian — asked me if I could pass them on to Miss Burt's next of kin. Burt-Ruckley, I suppose. I thought that next time I'm up at Wolfcleugh dig, I'll call in at the manor house and give them to him.'

Karen Stannard was looking at the photocopy of the newspaper cutting. 'I always think that passport photographs are so unlike reality. And when they're reproduced, such as here, they just look like death masks, don't they?' She frowned. 'Esoteric sort of study, I would have thought for Sally Burt.' She picked up the sheet, inspected it more closely. 'A missing black woman . . . 1981. I wonder what all that was about . . .'

She began to read from the cutting, aloud.

HAVE YOU SEEN THIS WOMAN?
Concern is being expressed about the mysterious disappearance of the mystery woman who checked into the George Hotel in Morpeth almost a week ago. She has not been seen for several days, after telling the staff on duty that she was taking a walk in the town. The woman was last seen boarding a bus for Berwick, but after that nothing has been heard of her.

Added to the mystery is the fact that she has left behind her in the hotel room all her personal possessions, including a passport which, it is understood, was issued in Italy. When last seen she was wearing a flowered dress and a light coat top. Police are calling for witnesses and are not prepared to say at this stage that foul play is suspected.

Karen shook her head. 'I wonder what Sally Burt found interesting in that little item. Still . . .' She replaced the cutting, picked up Arnold's Black Moor file and turned to leave. At the door she paused. 'That box file . . . no need for you to take it to Burt-Ruckley. Your *little friend* Portia, she's going up to see Diane Power at the Wolfcleugh dig today. Give it to her. She can call at the hall and hand it over to Burt-Ruckley then. Save you a trip. Got to keep your nose to the grindstone, haven't we, Arnold? Make sure you don't get up to any *mischief*.'

Arnold did not care for the emphasis she had placed on the words 'little friend' nor for the malicious glint in her eyes when she talked of mischief.

It possibly accounted for his brusqueness when he saw Portia in the staff canteen an hour later. 'I hear you're going up to Wolfcleugh this afternoon.'

'That's right.'

'I have some of Sally Burt's personal possessions. Karen suggests you might hand them over to Burt-Ruckley while you're up there.'

'No problem.' Her tone was bland, her features impassive. It was as though nothing had happened that afternoon up at Wolfcleugh Hill.

* * *

'So where do we stand right now?' Assistant Chief Constable Greyson asked.

Culpeper shifted uneasily in his chair. He felt disturbed when Greyson insisted on these meetings in a desire to be kept up to date with the current investigation. Culpeper was back on more familiar territory now: the general policing activity had turned into a murder investigation and this was more in line with the experience he had been honing over the last twenty years and more. He no longer felt like a fish out of water. But he disliked being regularly interrogated by the Assistant Chief Constable. It made him edgy. 'Well sir, if I begin with the forensic report that's come in from the labs. We now know that the young woman was struck down from behind. She put up no struggle. She went down and was struck probably another three times. It was deliberate murder. Secondly, we also know she was not killed at the place where she was found. She was transported there in some way or another. Then she was thrown down the slope until she reached the point where she was found. Scratches, post-mortem, on the body, the result of her fall,' he explained.

'Hm. And time of death?'

Culpeper grimaced. 'Dr Ferryman refuses to place a fixed time as yet, you know how they are, sir, these forensic pathologists at Gosforth. They insist that until they've done all the tests—'

'They're just doing their jobs properly, Culpeper,' the Assistant Chief Constable said, noting the irritation creeping into the Chief Inspector's tone and aware it might head in his own direction at any moment.

'Of course, sir. Anyway, another reason why we can rule out accident is that Ferryman reckons that while he can't be precise he's certain that death occurred during the evening prior to the mob attack on the protesters' camp at Wolfcleugh. Sally Burt was not struck down in the general melee at the camp. She was deliberately killed elsewhere and dumped in the woods, maybe in the hope she wouldn't be found, maybe trusting that it would be seen as a by-product of the fighting.'

'Which you don't think it was.'

'That's right, sir.'

'So, who are we looking at?' Greyson asked, leaning back in his chair and smoothing one hand along his right temple.

'We're discounting no one in our sights at the moment, sir. First of all, we know that Sally Burt probably had a relationship of some kind with Nick Semmens. There's no evidence it was sexual, though I think he might have wanted it to end up that way and they had been seen together in Newcastle, and he counts himself as a ladies' man—'

'Where is he at the moment?' the Assistant Chief Constable asked.

'We had to release him on bail,' Culpeper announced in a niggled tone. 'He tried to scarper south and we had him in the cells for questioning, but we had to let him go for the time being. We've let him know in no uncertain terms what will happen if he tries to do a runner again.'

'I don't like it, Culpeper.'

Neither do I, Culpeper snarled to himself, but what was to be done? Smart-arsed lawyers . . . 'So we still have Semmens in the frame, because he was seen up at the camp that evening. He had opportunity, therefore, though as to motive . . . well, it's a bit thin.'

'He wasn't seen with her at the camp?'

'Apparently not. But we do have this sequence. Sally Burt visited Burt-Ruckley at Wolfcleugh House late that afternoon. Family chat, it seems. Then she went down into the camp. Burt-Ruckley reckons she was going to see Semmens. We do know she certainly saw Jenny Farley and there's evidence that the two quarrelled.'

Greyson frowned, tugged at his lower lip with finger and thumb. 'About what?'

Culpeper shrugged. 'No direct evidence, but we can guess it might have had something to do with Semmens. It seems that our ponytailed stud had been in a close relationship with the Farley girl. She was pregnant by him. Sally Burt comes into camp, asking for Semmens. They have an argument — Jenny Farley probably tells her to stay away from her boyfriend. Sally Burt stalks off—'

'Presumably still looking for Semmens.'

'Seems so.'

'Maybe she found him.'

'It's a possibility. He denies it, but he might be lying. Maybe she found him, they discussed Jenny, who knows? Maybe it was Semmens who killed her, then took the opportunity later when the fighting started to dump her at the edge of the battle, hoping she'd be seen as part of it. But he claims he never saw her that night.'

'The Farley girl?'

Culpeper shrugged. 'She's a hard little madam; chip off the father's block, if you ask me. And she certainly had an argument with Sally Burt. So she could have followed Sally, clobbered her up there on the hill. But whether she'd have had the strength to drag her down into the woods—'

'Unless Semmens helped her. They could be in this together . . . if only in the disposal of the body.' The Assistant Chief Constable looked thoughtful. 'So, we can discount any blame or fault being laid at the door of Ken Stafford.'

Which was really why the Chief Constable had probably insisted to his assistant that these sessions should be held, Culpeper concluded. It was all about keeping things clean, not allowing any of his county friends to get uneasy, sweep away any dirt that might possibly besmirch their precious, pristine coat-tails.

'We can't exclude anyone at this stage, sir. I have my own views about how that ruckus started up there in the camp. I think Stafford's been under financial pressure. He got impatient with the delays. He wanted to put more pressure on the council. Or maybe it was just rage. Anyway, I'm convinced he set Colm Graham at it. Graham is Stafford's muscle; they've got a history that pair. If they don't get their own way, someone gets hurt. So Stafford gave Graham the nod; he gathered together a motley collection of hired thugs, some from among their own employees, and they went up there to Wolfcleugh to sort out what they would regard as the pansies in the wood.'

'But that doesn't put Stafford — or Graham for that matter — in the frame for the Burt murder. You said it couldn't be linked to the battle. She died before the fight started.'

Glowering, Culpeper was forced to agree. 'But I'm working on it, sir. One thing's for sure, anyway. I can't see Stafford standing a chance in hell as far as getting the Shangri-La development through is concerned now. He took a step too far, in his bloody arrogance. He's blown it, I reckon.'

'That's nothing to do with us,' the Assistant Chief Constable said coldly. 'So, is there anything else?'

Culpeper shrugged. 'There is, sir, as a matter of fact. We've got Nick Semmens in the frame, maybe his girlfriend Jenny, and maybe her old man Joe Farley too. He was seen up there in the woods during that period, using his own knuckles. But we've come across another odd bit of information. It seems that Sally Burt was under some kind of investigation herself.'

'I don't understand.'

'It's come to our attention that someone was making enquiries about her. At her digs and at the university.'

'The nature of the enquiry?'

'We don't know. But we do know the identity of the person asking the questions. He's called Dickson. He described himself as a private investigator.'

'Interesting . . .'

'It may be, when we trace him. But quite how long that will take . . .'

In fact it took less time than Culpeper had supposed.

After he left the Assistant Chief Constable's office he walked down the stairs and along the corridor to his own room. He was met there by Detective Inspector Farnsby. There was a triumphant, self-satisfied gleam in Farnsby's eyes. 'That guy Dickson, sir. He's in reception. Says he's heard we're looking for him. So he's here.'

'So what are we waiting for?' Culpeper rumbled.

* * *

In the starkness of the interview room, with a large uniformed policeman standing by, Dickson looked small, insignificant and seedily nervous. He was in his mid-fifties, Culpeper guessed; his blue suit had a shiny look to it and the shirt of his collar had a grey tinge from numerous washings. He was almost bald, long hair at the side being slicked across in a vain attempt to hide his baldness and his eyes were furtive, flickering this way and that, never resting their glance at one point for any length of time.

'Mr Dickson,' Culpeper said heavily. 'We been looking for you.'

'So I gather. There was a message at my office—'

'You operate out of Teesside.'

'That's right. Private enquiries. Discreet investigations.'

'So what was your interest in Sally Burt?'

'I beg your pardon?' The little man looked surprised. 'I didn't have any interest in her. She—'

'Wait a minute.' Culpeper was tired and irritable. Meetings with the Assistant Chief Constable affected him that way. 'Let's get things on the table right at the start. We're grateful you've come in of your own volition, as soon as you heard we were out looking for you. Very public-spirited for sure. But let's be clear that we don't have time to mess around. We're conducting a murder investigation here. Sally Burt is dead and we intend finding the person who killed her. And we think you can help. All right?'

Dickson swallowed nervously. His Adam's apple bobbed up and down, frantic. 'Of course, I'll do anything I can to help. But I'm not sure—'

'We can begin with your telling us who it was — the name of the person who took you on to make enquiries about Sally Burt. Then we can talk about the nature of those enquiries.'

Dickson's features were blank. He licked his lips nervously. 'I'm afraid there's been some kind of mistake here.'

'Let's hope you're not the one making it, bonny lad, by giving us the run-around,' Culpeper warned.

'No, no, you don't seem to understand. We're at cross purposes here. I wasn't making enquiries about Sally Burt. I was making enquiries *for* her!'

Culpeper scowled. 'She employed you? But you went to her digs. You called at the university. You asked about her—'

'Ah, you must understand. She first got in touch with me by phone; asked me to do this work for her. It wasn't all that difficult actually, once you know what you're looking for. Not difficult.' He shrugged uncertainly, passing a nervous hand over his bald head. 'Though not particularly conclusive, either.'

'So why did you call at her lodgings?'

'I was unable to raise her by phone. I used the number she'd given me. She seemed to be away. But I had the information — such as it was — that she requested and I happened to be in the area, so I called at the address she'd given me. The landlady directed me to the university. I called at the general office and then at the library. She wasn't there, so I left a message. The following day I caught up with her and gave her the information I'd obtained.'

Culpeper frowned. 'And just what was this information?'

Dickson shifted in his seat uneasily. 'These things are confidential to the client, of course—'

'Your client has been murdered,' Culpeper snarled.

'And I haven't been paid, you know,' Dickson whined.

Culpeper leaned forward. 'If you don't get on with it, you'll get the kind of payment you certainly won't want to receive. What was the information you gave to Sally Burt? Who did it concern?'

Dickson teased his lips with his tobacco-stained teeth. 'She asked me to find out what I could about a black woman called Joan Fevers. Well, she was actually called Juanita Veira. Or so I found out. Her Italian passport was in the name of Joan Fevers. But I was actually able to trace her quite easily. Not least because she had a police record.'

'Fevers . . . Veira . . . ?' Culpeper's temper was rising. 'Just who was this woman?'

'She was an Argentinian prostitute, or ex-prostitute. Whatever . . .' Dickson's voice trailed away uncertainly.

'Why the hell was Sally Burt interested in an Argentinian ex-prostitute?' Culpeper wondered.

Dickson shrugged. 'She didn't tell me. But, you know, we professionals—'

Culpeper was displeased by the implied linkage in the *we*.

'Professionals in this line of work, we soon begin to perceive what's behind the enquiry. So once I'd got the information, and asked myself what reason Miss Burt might have for her enquiry, I did a bit more digging, got some other information, certificates of birth and marriage and . . . well, I think I have a sort of picture, a sort of idea what it's all about—'

'Tell me,' Culpeper growled, and sat and listened while the little enquiry agent talked.

Arnold worked at his desk for most of the afternoon. He felt edgy, ill at ease with himself. He was unable to determine the reason for his edginess. He had tried not to dwell on the end of the evening with Karen Stannard and felt he had come to terms with the coolness of his relationship with Portia. But some of the pleasure he had always obtained from working in the department had been dissipated.

He needed to get out.

He went through the files on his desk. It was some time since he had visited the site up at Dorthgill, near the deserted village of Tynehead. He could go up there now, take the opportunity to clear his head in the breezes that whirled above the little valley below Tynehead Fell. The watershed at the two rivers there was so close that the rivers almost touched at their source and in the midwinter storms it was sometimes impossible to determine whether the water was coming or going — east to the Tees, or essaying the long journey north to mingle with the waters of the Tyne.

There had been a small team up there, at the old mine workings, a group from Sunderland University. Time he called on them to check on their progress. He went down to the car park, unlocked the car. It would be pleasant up there, high on the fells.

His mobile phone rang. For a moment he thought he would ignore it. Then he checked who was ringing.

'Arnold? Is that you?'

'Portia. What can I do for you?' His tone was deliberately cool.

'I'm up at Wolfcleugh . . . at the dig. The box file I picked up from you. Sally Burt's. I took it along to Wolfcleugh House but there was no one there. I didn't think I should just leave it on the porch, so I brought it along with me here, at the dig.'

Arnold waited. He could hear Portia breathing. She seemed somewhat agitated. 'So what's the problem?'

'Well, I was here and Diane Power was busy. I had nothing to do until she arrived so . . . I took a look at some of the stuff in the box.'

Just as Karen Stannard had, Arnold thought. Feminine curiosity. Insatiable. 'You should just give it to Burt-Ruckley,' he advised.

'Well, yes, I intend to. But Arnold . . . I looked at the stuff in there and there's some strange information. I can't quite make head or tail of it—'

'I don't think it's any of our business, Portia,' he warned.

'I know.' There was uncertainty in her voice, a certain nervousness. 'It's just that, well, I don't really want to go along to give it to Burt-Ruckley. Not alone.'

'Why not?'

'It's . . . I don't know . . . I'd rather you came with me. Arnold, would you mind? Can you get up here? I'm at the site. I'll wait for you. We can give it to Burt-Ruckley together . . .'

After she had rung off and Arnold was driving north to Wolfcleugh he was still arguing with himself as to why he had agreed. She was being foolish about something, he was certain, but she was clearly on edge, nervous, and he felt he could not leave her in such a situation. It was to him that Georgina Hope had entrusted the package and perhaps it had been unfair to ask Portia to take it to Wolfcleugh House. Not that he could imagine where the problem lay. Burt-Ruckley had been shattered by Sally Burt's death; the very deterioration in his appearance demonstrated how badly he had been affected. That was probably why Portia was nervous: she had read something in Sally Burt's papers that would have been upsetting to Burt-Ruckley, something that would have caused him even more distress. She needed Arnold there with her to help her break the news.

Perhaps Arnold felt flattered at the thought that it was to him she had turned in her dilemma.

He crossed the high fell on the top road that gave him a faster route to Wolfcleugh. Up here where wet heath and patches of blanket mire straddled the open stony ground the migrating waders came, miles from the seashores: lapwing and golden plover, dunlin and snipe. The northern slopes were thronged in August with shooting parties, converging towards the stone and turf butts to harry the flurrying grouse. But now the moors were quiet and silent under the late afternoon sun as Arnold dropped into the valley that wound at the foot of Wolfcleugh Hill.

When he arrived at the site of the dig there was no sign of Portia's car. He wandered across to the small team working in the trench. 'Anything of note?' he asked.

The young university student brushed back a lock of fair hair and shook her head. 'Not a lot really. We recovered some pottery shards yesterday and a metal buckler. Nothing of any real significance. My guess is this site is worked out.'

The assured wisdom of the young. 'Is Dr Power around?'

'In the hut.'

Arnold walked across to the hut. Diane Power looked up as he entered. 'Arnold. Portia Tyrrel was trying to get hold of you.'

'She got hold of me. That's why I'm here. She wanted me to go up to Wolfcleugh House with her.'

'Oh. Well, I guess she decided she couldn't wait.' Diane Power came along to the entrance and looked up the hill towards the ravaged woods. 'She was here. Just hanging around, really. Then she asked me for my binoculars. She saw someone up on the hill. Just on the skyline up there.'

'Who was it?'

Diane Power shrugged her muscular shoulders and wiped grubby hands on her faded jeans. 'I don't know. I didn't pay much attention, to be honest. But there were two men up there, walking along the ridge.'

'Down towards Wolfcleugh House?'

'In that direction, yes.' She glanced at Arnold uncertainly. 'Portia seemed a bit . . . odd. Sort of tense. She was worried about something.'

Arnold nodded. 'Yes. That's why she called me. But where is she now?'

'I think she must have got tired of waiting. At least, after she saw the two people up there she gave me the binoculars back and then she drove off.'

'Where?'

'My impression is she was going up to Wolfcleugh House.'

Arnold frowned, turned, then hesitated, looked back to Dr Power. 'The people on the ridge. Was one of them a woman?'

'Like I said, I didn't pay much attention. And I didn't use the binoculars. But I think one of them was Mr Burt-Ruckley, anyway. Maybe Portia mentioned his name. I'm not sure . . . sorry I can't be of more help. Is there a problem?'

Arnold shrugged. 'I'll go on after her, up to Wolfcleugh House.'

Dr Power gave him a shrewd glance. 'I think she'd like that.'

Arnold walked back to his car and drove off the site, down to the side road that curved around the hill towards Wolfcleugh House. As he advanced up the drive he could see that Portia's car was there, parked on the gravelled drive near the main entrance. He left his own car just beyond hers and got out.

The house was silent. The front door stood ajar.

Arnold walked up the steps to the Georgian façade with its elaborate portico and hesitated. He put out his hand, pushed at the door. From somewhere within the house he thought he heard the sound of voices.

'Hello!' He called out but there was no answer. He walked across the tessellated floor of the hallway, guided by the sound of raised voices. Then, suddenly, everything changed. He heard shouting, a crash; a woman screamed high, panicked, and then there was another loud crash, echoing, reverberating through the house. The sound had come from the gunroom, beyond the library.

Arnold ran forward, his heart pounding in his chest.

The door to the gunroom was open: the smell of oil was now mingled with something much more pungent and smoke drifted, hanging in the air. He caught a brief glimpse of Portia standing beside the desk. She was holding her hands over her ears, screaming, but no sound was issuing from her mouth. Her eyes were shut tightly and there was something on her face and on her blouse, grey and red, a spreading stain, wetness.

There was a huddled figure behind her on the floor, beyond the desk, but Arnold's attention was swinging to the other person in the narrow room.

It was the stocky, muscular figure of Joe Farley. He was bellowing at the top of his voice, his eyes wild, his face suffused with anger and panic, and in his hands was a shotgun, its muzzle swinging in Arnold's direction.

For one long, frozen second the world seemed to stand still: Farley bellowing like an enraged bull, Portia, mouth wide open, silently screaming in horror as the blood and brain matter spattered her breast, the gun smoke blue and pungent in the confined air of the gunroom. Then instinctively Arnold charged forward. There was no question of thought or of discretion. He threw himself at Joe Farley, grabbing the shotgun, forcing it upwards to point at the ceiling, only for Farley to bring the stock around in a whirling

160

arc, striking Arnold across the shoulder, throwing him off balance, sending him staggering, lurching to the ground.

He retained his desperate grasp of the shotgun barrel and as he went down he pulled Farley with him. The older man was on top, breathing hard, wild-eyed, trying to shout something and tugging to drag the gun free from Arnold's grasp, but Arnold hung on desperately, as Portia found her voice at last again and screamed, a high, piercing note that exposed all the terror and panic and horror that had overtaken her. Farley was still dragging at the gun, his contorted features close to Arnold so he could smell the man's stale, frightened breath. He was almost seated astride Arnold and his twisted features made him nearly unrecognisable. His eyes were bulging, thick, worm-like veins corded his neck and his mouth was open and gasping. He still seemed to be trying to shout something but it was unintelligible to Arnold. He twisted sideways, Farley lost his balance and slid backwards, crashing into the desk behind which lay the man who had been Burt-Ruckley.

Dazed, Farley lost his grip on the shotgun. Arnold hit him with the edge of his hand, just below his nose, and Farley screamed with pain before his eyes glazed. He gasped, falling backwards, and Arnold tore the shotgun completely from his grasp.

He staggered to his feet. Farley was down, gasping, tears flowing from his eyes as he fought for breath, and from the corner of his eye Arnold caught a glimpse of Portia, wild-eyed, grabbing at her stained blouse. A red mist seemed to rise up in front of Arnold, red and black and vicious. The man at his feet was struggling for breath but a murderous fog was enveloping Arnold. He raised the shotgun, holding it by its barrel. He was aware of hands dragging at him, weak and feeble, but he ignored them, thrust them away, beat them off. Someone was screaming at him but he had raised his hands, the stock of the shotgun poised to smash into the face of the helpless man at his feet.

Hands beat at his shoulders, rained blows at his head and he staggered. The red mist began to fade, the words were getting through to him. He could make them out only faintly as though from a great distance and they hardly overcame the great roaring of blood in his head.

Then he realised it was Portia. Her eyes were panicked, her mouth contorted, her face streaked with tears of terror. But she was shouting at him, screaming the words over and over, until finally they beat their knifelike way into his violence-dulled brain. 'It's not him, Arnold! *For God's sake, it's not him!*

4

The house seemed to be full of people. There were policemen in their flat caps with their black and white chequered bands; there were men in suits and others in white jackets. The noise seemed like a tumult a miscegenation of noise and accents, a babbling of different tones and tongues, a Babel whirling around in Arnold's head. In the courtyard outside, through the open doors, he caught a glimpse of two police cars, an ambulance, a beating, whirling blue light. He staggered outside again into the fresh air; he was sick again, as he had been sick half an hour earlier.

When Portia had dragged him away from Joe Farley he had managed to calm down, if only to counteract the shaking hysteria that attacked her. He had found a rag on the desk and had begun to mop at her face and throat, removing the blood and the spattering of brain tissue. And as he had used the cloth with its gun oil stains to clean her, she was babbling at him, as his gorge rose with the smearing of blood and grey matter under his fingers.

'I saw them on the hill and I thought I didn't need to wait for you, I could come up here, give him Sally's papers. I knew he wouldn't be alone here. I didn't want to give them to him if he was alone. I was afraid that when he read them . . .'

'It's all right,' Arnold soothed. 'It's all right. It's all over now. You don't need to talk about it. You should have waited for me . . .'

'But I saw them on the hill,' she babbled on, 'and I thought it would be all right. I came up here just after they had arrived at the hall. They had just got in and I followed them into the hall; I heard them talking in the gunroom. That man was threatening him, his voice was angry. It was horrible. He was talking to Burt-Ruckley. I didn't know who he was, but I could guess, something Burt-Ruckley said. He was calm, you know, controlled. He was sitting behind his desk over there. He had the shotgun in his hands, broken up. He had taken it down from the rack . . . he was polishing it, calm . . . calm . . .'

She was shuddering. She would not have recognised Joe Farley. She hadn't seen him during the struggle at the Northumberland Arms, because she had remained in the lounge while Arnold had entered the main bar to drag Sally Burt away. A Sally Burt already under strain, because she knew things, suspected things . . .

'The man was standing in front of Burt-Ruckley and he was angry. He seemed to be threatening him. But he stopped speaking when I entered. And Burt-Ruckley looked up. He saw me, and he saw the box I was carrying and he must have guessed what it contained. He just sort of smiled at me, a sad smile, as though it was something he had been expecting a long time, with dread, and now it was here—'

She shook her head, gagging as Arnold wiped her face.

'They just stayed there, looking at me, and I didn't know what to say and then I just put the box file on his desk and said it belonged to Sally. I was bringing the papers to him. I think he must have known already, maybe from my face, known what was in the box. And then he just looked at this man standing in front of him and he said, "You see? It's already too late." Then he snapped closed the shotgun he'd been cleaning and lifted it . . .'

Arnold could see the start of panic in her eyes again and tried to soothe her. 'Quiet now, leave it for the moment . . .'

But the words came pouring out in a torrent of hysteria. 'He lifted it and this other man seemed petrified for a moment. He must have thought Burt-Ruckley was going to shoot him. He turned, grabbed at one of the other shotguns on the wall lifted it as though to protect himself, pointed it at Burt-Ruckley and pulled at the trigger, but the gun wasn't loaded. And all the time Burt-Ruckley was looking at him, smiling in the strangest way. Then it happened. He pulled the triggers of the gun he was holding, the gun he'd been polishing . . .'

It had been a double-barrelled shotgun.

She was babbling again, hysterical with the memory of it. 'He just pointed it and pulled. I saw him. He blew off almost all of the side of his own head.' Her eyes glazed again with the horror of it. Her voice dropped, almost whispering. 'It was like a red, disintegrating cloud of mist. It covered me. I felt it splashing on me. And I looked at myself and it was all over me. And I was screaming. But then I couldn't scream. And it was all over me, wet and dark and horrible. And I couldn't get a sound out and I shut my eyes, and there was shouting. And then when I opened my eyes again you were here and you were standing over that man. And I could see it in your face. You were crazy, out of your mind, ready to smash the gun into his face, make a bloody mess again, like Burt-Ruckley's head, and I grabbed you, hit you, screamed at you but it was as though you couldn't hear me, as though you were drugged . . .'

She was staring at him, her eyes wide, but calmer now, though deep in their darkness panic still stirred, seeking escape. 'You thought the man you were attacking was the one who had killed Burt-Ruckley. But he didn't kill him. Burt-Ruckley shot himself. Do you understand? He knew why I had come and he decided it was all over. He shot himself.' She began to moan, a low keening sound. 'Why did he do that?'

* * *

Later, when they all came rushing into the house and there was a flurry of orders and tramping of hurrying feet, Detective Chief Inspector Culpeper laid a hand on Arnold's shoulder. 'All right, you can leave her now. The ambulance is ready. She needs to go with them.' He took the stained cloth from Arnold's hand. It was already drying, streaked with dark blood, grey matter, gun oil.

Culpeper's grip on his shoulder tightened, as Arnold shook his head wordlessly, unwilling to release the shuddering woman in his arms. 'Let her go now and you come through here with me. I'll get you down to the hospital myself in a little while, but you'd better rest first, calm down.'

They went into the drawing room and Arnold collapsed in an easy chair. From somewhere, Culpeper produced a glass of whisky, gave it to Arnold. The fierce liquid burned his throat and he coughed.

Culpeper sat there quietly, facing him, saying nothing. Then, some ten minutes later, after the ambulance had gone, the policeman took Arnold out to the car helped him into the back seat. They drove back down the country lanes and on to the A1, south to Morpeth.

Arnold was hardly aware of the countryside passing by. All he could see was what was in his mind's eye: gun smoke, blood spatter and a red mist as he roared himself on to smash a shotgun stock into a helpless man's face.

And all he could hear was the screaming.

* * *

'A messy end,' the Assistant Chief Constable suggested with a grimace of distaste. 'Is she all right now?'

'They released her from hospital yesterday. Shock, really. An unpleasant, frightening experience. It'll be giving Miss Tyrrel nightmares for a while I've no doubt,' Culpeper agreed.

Assistant Chief Constable Greyson frowned. 'I assume she'd read the papers in the box file. Had she worked out the implications, what it was all about?' he asked.

Culpeper shook his head. 'I don't reckon so, not completely. But it seems she'd read enough of the information among Sally Burt's papers, with that supplied by our little investigative friend Dickson, to begin to get a hazy idea of what it was all about. The newspaper cutting; a copy of a birth certificate in the name of Steven Palmer, two marriage certificates, both carrying the same name. Steven Palmer and Amanda Burt-Ruckley. Steven Palmer and Joan Fevers. And she could see the dates on the certificates. She could make an educated guess and she knew there might be trouble when she gave the papers to Burt-Ruckley. That's why she rang Landon, asked him to go to the house with her. But when she saw Burt-Ruckley on the hill, with another man — Farley — she decided she would not be alone with Burt-Ruckley and that it would be okay to go alone, without waiting for Landon. Bad mistake. Stupid thing to do.'

'Impatience? Curiosity?'

Culpeper shrugged. 'Bit of both, I would say. She knew Sally Burt, liked her. She knew the girl had been under some kind of strain. Maybe she wanted to see Burt-Ruckley's face when he received the papers. When he realised that she could guess what it was all about.'

'If she hadn't gone up there, maybe Burt-Ruckley wouldn't have pulled the trigger on himself,' Greyson mused.

'If not then, it would have been another time,' Culpeper suggested. 'For Burt-Ruckley her coming there was the last straw. Farley had already cottoned on to some of it. Now Miss Tyrrel. It was something he had been dreading for twenty years. His world was coming crashing down. I suppose he felt it was time to end it.'

'I don't suppose we'll ever be able to piece everything together,' the Assistant Chief Constable wondered.

Culpeper shrugged. 'I think we have enough. The woman, the black woman in the case, she was an Argentinian ex-prostitute called Juanita Veira, who had a false Italian passport in the name of Joan Fevers. We've been able to establish she'd been arrested in Italy on drug charges, jumped bail and got into England illegally. Quite how and where she met the young Steven Palmer we'll never know, but maybe he used her once or twice, in a professional capacity as a lonely young man on the streets, who knows. Anyway, he was down on his luck, he needed money, so he agreed with her pimp to go through a marriage of convenience, to give her a British nationality and passport. That was in 1979. And that was that, really. I imagine he never thought he'd see her again.'

'But then he got married,' Greyson murmured. 'That's right. To a woman working in an advertising agency. A cut above him, really, because as far as we can make out Steven Palmer's background was East End. He'd worked hard at his accent . . . Anyway, he met Amanda Burt-Ruckley. It was probably love — or at least we can be charitable enough to believe so. They got married in 1981. Then, not long afterwards, his luck really turned. Her uncle died, childless, she succeeded to the Northumberland estates and suddenly he was a rich man. Trouble was, there was a fair bit of publicity about it.'

'Advertising girl inherits landed estates.'

'That sort of thing, yes, sir.'

'And the Argentinian ex-prostitute saw his picture in the newspapers?'

Culpeper nodded. 'Most probably. And she saw her chance. She was after money, of course. She came north, booked into the George Hotel in Morpeth and . . . disappeared. There was a brief flurry of interest in the newspapers, but it soon died down when she became just another missing person. The Italian passport was in her room and that raised a few problems, but eventually it was all forgotten.'

'Burt-Ruckley?'

'The guess is he killed her. He'd changed his name from Palmer to Burt-Ruckley and he was about to live the life of a landed gentleman, with a loving wife, great estates, as much money as he could ever need. And then this whore turned up, threatening to expose the fact that he was a bigamist and that his marriage to Amanda had never been a marriage. You can imagine what the papers would have made of that. So we can assume he killed her. We think he buried her in the woods, up at Wolfcleugh.'

'The remains that Miss Tyrrel found . . . ?'

Culpeper nodded. 'We think it was her. A bit of her, at least. Whether we'll ever prove it is another matter. Not really enough forensic to go on.'

Greyson sighed. 'And after that, he had almost twenty years of silence and peace.'

Culpeper was not so sure. Not long after he had killed the ex-prostitute, Amanda Burt-Ruckley had died in a show-jumping accident. And there he was, with the estate all to himself. He enjoyed it, certainly, but Culpeper suspected he had never come to enjoy peace there. Always, at the back of his mind, there would have been the gnawing doubt, the anxiety that one day it might all come out, that she would be found in her grave in the woods.

'He kept to himself,' Culpeper agreed. 'Lived a life of ease and plenty. And got very used to it. And maybe over the years he had become relaxed. Until one day Sally Burt walked into his life, announcing she was part of the family.'

'Do you think he saw it as a problem, initially?'

'Hard to say, sir. There's a view he genuinely liked her. On the other hand, maybe he invited her up there to keep an eye on her, make sure she didn't cause him any problems. Because Sally was a New World person: she had no background she knew of, she wanted to know where she had come from. And she asked him questions, began to probe. Maybe he was a bit dismissive. Anyway, she was sufficiently interested to dig a little deeper. And soon some puzzling things emerged. The Palmer-Burt-Ruckley marriage was one thing, but she took the additional step of looking him up as well. And there was a marriage celebrated in London between Steven Palmer and one Joan Fevers. Celebrated two years prior to marriage with Amanda. She was puzzled and a bit scared. It could mean that Steven Burt-Ruckley's had been a bigamous marriage. He would then not be entitled to

Wolfcleugh and the next in line, therefore, would be Sally herself.'

She would probably not have been terribly happy at the thought, Culpeper guessed privately. It would have been a shock and possibly not a welcome one. She was a young New Zealander, looking for a future, certainly, but not seeking landed estates. Perhaps that was why, at that stage, she had engaged the private investigator Dickson, to get another view, confirm the facts or show her where she was going wrong. His confirmation would have worried her. But he also had something else. Joan Fevers had become a missing person — after coming north, probably to confront Burt-Ruckley.

She had needed to talk to someone, before confronting Burt-Ruckley. That's where Culpeper had been misled, of course, in the timing of it all. Burt-Ruckley had told him Sally had visited him and *then* gone down to the camp. In fact, he had lied: the reverse had been true. Sally had gone to the camp to talk to Semmens, with whom she was friendly, maybe to get some advice, or support from him. But she had missed him. Instead, she'd met and quarrelled with Jenny Farley. It was after that she had gone up to Wolfcleugh and told Burt-Ruckley of her suspicions.

He had lied later, to Culpeper, making out she had seen him before going down to the woods to look for Semmens and to her death.

'It's why he killed her, of course,' the Assistant Chief Constable agreed. 'It would have been the end of his life as a gentleman. Are we going to be able to piece together the forensics in all this?'

'I think so. We still have no murder weapon — he probably ditched it in the woods. But we have traces of blood on a small tractor at Wolfcleugh. Looks like he struck from behind, killed her, then later that night loaded her on to the tractor, drove her up to the woods, pitched her down the slope. Next morning the battle started. She was already dead then.'

'Did you see him as a killer, when you met?' Culpeper grimaced. Did anyone ever *see* a killer before the event? 'I think he was a man who was coming to the end of his tether. He murdered the Argentinian woman twenty years ago to save his marriage and his lifestyle. I think he had difficulty living with that; maybe it accounted in part for his reclusive nature. Sally Burt's arrival was a shock and I think he must always have been worried that she'd find out something. And when she did he killed again — but it unnerved him. His past was creeping up on him. In the end, he could face no more.'

Culpeper thought back to the scene at Wolfcleugh.

Alerted to Sally Burt's findings by Dickson, they had gone up to Wolfcleugh to interview Burt-Ruckley to find a scene of carnage: blood everywhere, a hysterical woman covered in gore, Landon trying to clean her, Burt-Ruckley dead with half his head blown away and Joe Farley still dazed, an unloaded shotgun beside him.

'What exactly was Farley up to?' the Assistant Chief Constable asked. 'Do we do him for something as well?'

Culpeper shrugged. 'If you feel it worthwhile, sir. Fact is, when Sally went looking for Semmens in the woods she had a shouting match with the jealous girlfriend. She must have let slip why she wanted to talk to Semmens, telling the girl that it was nothing to do with Nick Semmens himself and her relationship with him. Whatever she said, Jenny Farley put two and two together. She was pregnant, she knew Nick Semmens wanted away and she talked to her father, Joe. They thought that if they put some pressure on Burt-Ruckley — even though they only had a glimmer of what it was all about — they could get some money out of it.'

'Blackmail?'

'Looks like: Farley met Burt-Ruckley on the ridge. He must have hinted he had some information that was worthwhile to Burt-Ruckley. They walked back to Wolfcleugh House. Farley put his proposition to Burt-Ruckley in the gunroom, where Burt-Ruckley was preparing to clean a gun. Maybe Burt-Ruckley would have gone along with it, maybe not. He was under strain: several people can give evidence of his physical deterioration — though they put it down to grief. Then in walks Miss Tyrrel. She tells him she's got papers belonging to Sally. That was it. I understand he said something to Farley about it all being too late. He even smiled in relief.'

'I suppose Farley thought Burt-Ruckley was about to shoot him.'

'Absolutely. When he saw him snap the breech closed, Farley panicked, grabbed a gun himself. It wasn't loaded. Then Burt-Ruckley pulled the triggers on himself and Landon came roaring into the room, assuming it was Farley who had fired. It all got very confused just then . . .'

If they had only arrived half an hour sooner, Culpeper thought, things could have been different. For Burt-Ruckley, for Landon and the young woman. But she'd get over it in time. As for Landon . . . he was lucky he wouldn't be facing a serious charge. Apparently, he'd been close to killing Farley in a blind rage.

Culpeper wondered about that . . .

5

Blind rage.

Arnold wondered about that. He walked along the hill where he had walked with Portia that day and he wondered about the red mist that had enveloped his senses when he had seen her silently screaming and saw the shotgun in Joe Farley's hands. What had driven him to such madness? Fury and revenge because he thought Farley had attacked Portia, was about to murder her as he seemed to have murdered Burt-Ruckley?

Perhaps it didn't pay to dwell upon it. Perhaps he didn't want to know the answer. He had to work with Portia Tyrrel and then there was Karen Stannard too. Just as he could never work out the colour of her eyes, so he guessed he would never get to understand what went on in her mind. Maybe he was just destined to stumble along, a mere male, not really understanding . . .

He walked on down the hill, back to the Wolfcleugh dig and the trench. It was unclear what was to happen to the Wolfcleugh estates now. *Bona vacantia*, perhaps, which would mean ownership by the Crown in the end. Maybe then a clearance for extension of the Moss investigations into Wolfcleugh Woods would be possible. One thing was certain. Keith Stafford's plan for Shangri-La was finished. The council had taken its courage in its hands and finally thrown out the argument for the access road. There was doubt now cast over the whole development. And about Ken Stafford's financial standing in Shangri-La Enterprises Ltd.

As Arnold crossed the rutted edge of the woods, where Farley had driven his bulldozer to attack the protesters led by Nick Semmens, he paused and looked about him. Somewhere among these trees, twenty years ago, Steven Burt-Ruckley had buried the woman whom he had married and who had returned to blackmail him. He must have been in an agony of doubt when the Shangri-La development access road was first mooted. He was terrified that once work started, some workman might chance upon the remains of the ex-prostitute he had married. It accounted for his ambivalence. He did not want anyone rooting through those woods, not Stafford's workmen, not Diane Power's archaeological team. But he seemed unable to control events. He tried to use the protesters, he tried to use Arnold's department; but each way he wriggled he still faced the same difficulty, the same danger.

And finally there was the problem of Sally Burt. Innocently enough, she was merely seeking her family background, trying to discover her roots. But she was a danger and he had reacted. Only to find the danger was still lurking there, as it had always done, since that dark day twenty years ago.

Arnold grunted, turned and went on his way down the hill. His movement disturbed a magpie, standing at the edge of the rut. It flew off alone. *One for sorrow, two for joy*, Arnold thought.

The magpie knew nothing of such old aphorisms. It remained in the trees for a little while, watchful, cocking its head on one side, waiting. Then, when the woods were all quiet again it took off, launched itself, planed in a handsome flash of black and white plumage down to the rutted ground once more. It moved quickly over the broken earth, returning to the spot where it had earlier found its prize.

The gold ring gleamed in the sunlight that came filtering through the trees. It was still attached to the dark-skinned, desiccated hand half buried in the earth, but the predatory beak of the magpie found that no problem. A few quick pecks at the exposed finger and the hard tissue flaked away, the black, peat-preserved skin was loosened and the ring dropped.

The magpie picked it up and flew off as greedy for gold as its black-skinned owner had been, twenty years ago.

THE END

ALSO BY ROY LEWIS

ERIC WARD MYSTERIES
Book 1: THE SEDLEIGH HALL MURDER
Book 2: THE FARMING MURDER
Book 3: THE QUAYSIDE MURDER
Book 4: THE DIAMOND MURDER
Book 5: THE GEORDIE MURDER
Book 6: THE SHIPPING MURDER
Book 7: THE CITY OF LONDON MURDER
Book 8: THE APARTMENT MURDER
Book 9: THE SPANISH VILLA MURDER
Book 10: THE MARRIAGE MURDER
Book 11: THE WASTEFUL MURDER
Book 12: THE PHANTOM MURDER
Book 13: THE SLAUGHTERHOUSE MURDER
Book 14: THE TATTOO MURDER
Book 15: THE FOOTBALL MURDER
Book 16: THE TUTANKHAMUN MURDER
Book 17: THE ZODIAC MURDER

INSPECTOR JOHN CROW
Book 1: A LOVER TOO MANY
Book 2: ERROR OF JUDGMENT
Book 3: THE WOODS MURDER
Book 4: MURDER FOR MONEY
Book 5: MURDER IN THE MINE
Book 6: A COTSWOLDS MURDER
Book 7: A FOX HUNTING MURDER
Book 8: A DARTMOOR MURDER

ARNOLD LANDON MYSTERIES
Book 1: MURDER IN THE BARN
Book 2: MURDER IN THE MANOR
Book 3: MURDER IN THE FARMHOUSE
Book 4: MURDER IN THE STABLE YARD
Book 5: MURDER IN THE CHURCH